LAUGH, CRY, CRITICIZE

100+ FLASH FICTION STORIES

By

Chris W. Schmidt

First published in 2025 by:

Books Publisher Hub
2029 Century Park East
Los Angeles, CA 90067
United States of America

ISBN (eBook): 978-1-968745-15-8
ISBN (Paperback): 978-1-968745-16-5
ISBN (Hardcover): 978-1-968745-17-2

Book Cover Art by Books Publisher Hub
Book Cover Design by Books Publisher Hub
Book Cover Styling by Books Publisher Hub

Printed and bound in the United States of America

Dedication

To my wife, Julie, who's supported me in everything I've done since the days of Gerald Ford.

To my family, who know all my flaws and still love me unconditionally.

To my friends, colleagues, acquaintances, and patients—thank you for, perhaps unwittingly, encouraging my storytelling.

And finally, to my late friend George Chin, Jr., who continues to inspire me.

Acknowledgment

My wife, Julie, by far my harshest critic.

My friends, Mark Worth, Steve Mosier, and Ray Mirly, who reviewed rough drafts and offered constructive criticism.

CONTENTS

About the Author

Chris W. Schmidt was born and raised in a small town in southwestern Iowa. He earned his medical degree from the University of Iowa and completed his residency training in San Francisco.

Following service in the U.S. Army, he went on to practice medicine for nearly forty-five years. Now retired, he lives with his wife in a vibrant retirement community in Arizona. They are the proud parents of four grown sons and grandparents to eight grandchildren.

Laugh, Cry, Criticize is his debut book. He fell in love with the flash fiction genre—it suits his short attention span perfectly.

Preface

Think of a novel as a gallon of ice cream, and a flash fiction story as a single lick of an ice cream cone. Sometimes you crave the whole gallon; other times, just a taste is enough.

The stories that follow offer only a glimpse—a sliver of narrative—leaving space for the reader's imagination to fill in the blanks. Because of this, each reader may interpret the stories differently. The author may have a vision of what the ambiguous elements mean, but there are no right or wrong answers.

Not every story will appeal to everyone. The collection spans a range of topics, from light to serious, and a few that are just a little strange.

Many—but not all—of these pieces are loosely inspired by the author's personal experiences. Think of them like those movies labeled "based on actual events": rooted in reality, but generously embellished.

What defines each story is its brevity. Most take only a minute or two to read. There's no continuity between them—no required order. Pick up the book, read a story, put it down, and return later. Perfect for when you have minutes rather than hours to spare.

And finally, don't take any of this too seriously. This isn't "literature" with a capital L. These are stories meant to distract, amuse, or occasionally provoke thought—but not to preach or teach. To borrow from Lincoln, "People will little note, nor long remember what is written here."

But hopefully, they'll enjoy the time spent here.

1: Honesty

"I'm not particularly proud of what I do for a living, but I am proud of how well I do it. A scam artist, a fraud, a cheat, a thief: yes, I confess to being all those things. However, I do not consider myself to be a bad person. In many ways, I am a good person. At various times, I have been a good son, a good brother, a good husband, a good father, a good friend, a good partner, and even a good neighbor. Not consistently, but still … at times.

I am currently working in the personal services industry. I am the founder and managing partner of the Psychic Consultation Network. I train and supervise 30 associate psychics who provide personalized readings for over five thousand clients each month. Clients are billed by the minute through a 900-number platform, ensuring a steady revenue stream for the network. It is a very lucrative venture, but of course, our reward is in the service we provide.

My career has followed a long and tortuous path with multiple forks and dead ends. I harbor no delusion that my current endeavor will persist for the long-term. Most likely, I will offer one of my associate psychics the opportunity to purchase the business. In my experience, it is best to divest from a cash cow when she is still giving cream. The key is in recognizing when that is. So, in summary, I am a businessman. Perhaps not in the traditional sense, but I am a successful entrepreneur nonetheless."

The teacher slowly rose from her chair. "Thank you, Mr. Smith. That was … certainly informative. And … unique."

She turned to the class, "Does anyone have a question for Tommy's dad?"

A dozen hands shot up at once.

2: Melancholia

Melancholia wrapped her arms tightly around him and pressed her lips cunningly against his. Their lips formed a sinister seal as she withdrew every dream and pleasure from within him. All that had been and all that might have been dissipated into the vapor of the embrace. Then she released him. He fell, a transparent form, unwilling to stand.

Those who encountered him observed no substance. He was not warmed by sunshine or refreshed by water. Nourishment was taken only begrudgingly, and sleep was his incessant refuge. He sought neither companionship nor conversation. In essence, he was no longer of this world.

It was not always so; once he had been bright and energetic. A never-ending stream of ideas darted forth, some finding fertile ground, others withering away. His talent and enthusiasm brought him success on many levels, achieving respect, friendship, prosperity, and love. There was always another goal, another challenge. This was a life of confidence and proven achievement.

It shattered in an instant. Without warning, he saw himself clearly and realized that he had failed. Not once had he done his best; always, he had done just enough to get by. He could have been a better student, athlete, worker, son, brother, friend, husband, or father. Lives would have been richer if only he had made the effort to live up to his potential. Now it was too late. He had damaged everything he had touched. There was no going back. Self-pity transformed into self-loathing.

Years passed. Those who had once loved him fell away. His achievements and reputation were forgotten. His name was no longer spoken. His surroundings became cold, dark, and isolated. Physical neglect didn't just surround him; it defined him. Had he died, no one would have noticed or cared.

Except he didn't die. Some cruel devil kept him alive to suffer in his existence. In his eighth decade, he gazed up from his chair and spotted a well-worn volume of the works of Edgar Allan Poe on a bookshelf. If ever there was a more miserable soul than himself, it was surely Poe. In those poems and short stories, his mind drifted into a world beyond his own. He traveled to the moon and cringed under a deadly pendulum. He pondered the genius of Monsieur Dupin and envisioned the beauty of Annabel Lee. Still isolated and detached, he was once again engaged.

Each morning, he rose with a purpose, reading everything in his library by or about Poe. Cautiously at first, then with rediscovered confidence, he ventured to the public library. He read, he analyzed, he speculated, and he developed a relationship with a man who had died a hundred years before he was born.

His touch could not damage Poe.

The sting of Melancholia's kiss began to fade.

3: The Kid

She was just a kid, about eight or nine years old. She wore a T-shirt, shorts, a ball cap, and rubber boots that came nearly to her knees. She carried an old cane pole in one hand, twice as long as she was tall, and a battered five-gallon bucket with all her tackle in the other.

Standing at the bank of the lake, she set the bucket down and took out a soup can filled with moist soil and nightcrawlers. She threaded a worm onto the hook, clamped the split shot on the line, and tied a cork bobber about two feet from the hook.

The line made a "plop" as it hit the water. Her eyes watched the bobber as she felt in her pocket for a piece of gum. Just as she was ready to unwrap it, the bobber dipped, and she lifted the pole to set the hook. A large bluegill emerged and was swung smoothly to the shore. She grasped the fish with her index finger through one of the gills and her thumb in the mouth as she removed the hook.

The bucket, half full of water, received the catch. She finished unwrapping the Juicy Fruit and smiled at the gush of flavor from the first chew. She checked the worm and plopped the line back in the water.

All this was observed by a couple of older men fishing a short distance away. Between them, there was nearly a thousand dollars' worth of rods, reels, and tackle. Yet after nearly an hour, they still hadn't caught a single fish.

The kid pulled in fish after fish. Bluegills, crappie, and even a smallmouth bass all went into the bucket. All the while, the old guys cast and cast with only minimal success.

Her bucket full, the kid struggled to lift her load as she headed for home. Passing the veteran anglers, she nodded and smiled.

"That kid can fish," they whispered in unison.

4: A Beginning

A nameless rider in the night announced the alert: "The regulars are coming out." Neighbor to neighbor, the word was disseminated. Each man knew what to do and where to go. This is what they had trained for, and they were ready.

A chilling, dawn mist clung to the fields as he gripped his musket tightly. He stood among his fellow Minutemen on Lexington Green, his heart pounding out of sync with the rhythm of the approaching British drums.

Yesterday, he had been untroubled, just a free black man digging an outhouse trench. Now, he stood in opposition to a well-trained army, perhaps to die.

But why? Liberty, but what did that even mean? He owned no land; he had no trade or livelihood threatened by the British. His life was unaffected.

Duty perhaps. He had joined the militia and trained as a minuteman in a patriotic fervor to protect his neighbors, but what threat were they facing? Why make a stand here? He couldn't break ranks, though he desperately wanted to. Then he whispered the most fervent prayer of his life.

He could hear the approach of the Redcoats before he could see them, an intimidating cacophony of drums, boots, and steel.

"Stand your ground!" came the command. "Don't fire unless fired upon!"

On they came. He stood in breathless silence, musket at the ready against his shoulder. His anxiety escalated with each step as they advanced.

"Bugger this," he thought. "There's no way I can miss from this distance."

His single shot rang out, and suddenly the air was alive with the first volley of musket fire. Thick black smoke filled his lungs and obscured his vision. He fired blindly into the chaos. Unexpectedly, he felt as if he had been clubbed with the butt of a musket and as if his chest were on fire. There was blood in his mouth, choking him. A giant weight prevented him from taking a breath.

The British surged forward, and his Captain called the retreat. The Redcoats flooded the green. He was faintly aware that his comrades had abandoned him, running for the cover of the woods.

His last thoughts were of the futility of the whole thing, "We accomplished nothing..."

He never knew that his was the *shot heard round the world.*

5: The Killer

The deputy approached the cell with a tray of food. He handed it through the slot and sat on a stool across from the cell to watch the prisoner eat.

"Doc, can I ask you a question?" the deputy asked uneasily.

"What's on your mind, Jimmy?" the prisoner replied.

"I was just wondering how you can kill a man. Doesn't it bother you?"

"Well, Jimmy, suppose when you brought that tray in for me, you found me standing outside this cell with a gun. What would you do?"

"I'd level my gun on you and tell you to drop yours and get back in the cell," said Jimmy.

Doc looked at Jimmy earnestly. "If you walked in and found me like that, I'd shoot you before you said a word. I would step over your dying body, walk out that door, and never give it another thought.

"Jimmy, you've been decent to me, treating me with human kindness. I had a son once, who would have been about your age if he'd lived. I'm going to give you some advice, like a father to a son.

"I'm a hard man, Jimmy. And a hard man only holds a gun to get what he wants. Only a fool gets in the way of me and what I want.

"Jimmy, you're a soft man. That's not a bad thing—it's just who you are. You're no more cut out to be a deputy than I am to be an opera singer. It's dangerous work. Sooner or later, you're going to come up against a hard man, and if you stand between him and what he wants, you'll get shot."

Doc paused and took a sip of coffee. His eyes fixated on Jimmy's.

"You better pray that he shoots you in the heart. Then dying will be quick. If he shoots you in the lungs, you'll slowly choke on your own blood. It'll take several minutes and will hurt like Hell.

"God help you if he shoots you in the gut. Then you'll linger for anywhere from a day to a week. There's nothing that can be done. The pain will be unbearable—the thirst, even worse."

Jimmy looked away, his mouth agape.

"When the sheriff gets back, put that badge on his desk. Say, 'Thank you and goodbye,' and walk out that door. Don't let him bully you or shame you into staying. Walk down the street and get a job as a clerk in a store. In time, you'll find a sweetheart and probably have a family. Walk away, and you'll likely die in your bed, surrounded by people who care. Keep that badge on your chest, and there's nothing good in your future."

"What did you say to him?" the sheriff asked the prisoner as Jimmy walked out.

"Just that the food here is better than most," Doc replied.

6: Bifocals

The waitress lingered at the diner counter as the man struggled with the laminated menu. He moved the menu back and forth, trying to focus. Finally, he took his glasses off. He assumed an awkward position with his head tilted forward and turned slightly to the right.

"I'll have the number three breakfast," he announced.

"You got it," she replied. Then, against her better judgment, she said, "Honey, have you ever tried bifocals?"

"Cain't wear bifocals—I drive truck," he stated as if that made perfect sense.

Her immediate reaction was amusement. Surely, he was joking. "You'll have to explain that one to me," she said with a pleasant smile.

"They blurry the road when I tilt my head back to take a sip of beer," was his reply.

She carefully studied his face; there wasn't a twitch or hint of a smirk. This guy was good; he was playing it straight. "Now I *know* you're pulling my leg. I've been waiting tables since high school, and that is a first. I don't know how you can say that with a straight face."

He seemed genuinely confused. "You ever try lookin' through a bifocal at something far away?"

The blood rushed to her face. He wasn't joking! Her smile stiffened. How in the world did he get a commercial driver's license?

She served his breakfast and could hardly wait for him to finish and leave. As soon as he climbed into his rig, she reached for the phone. Today, she would do the right thing.

A short while later, the State Patrol pulled over a semi for an improper lane change on the Interstate. The driver passed the breathalyzer test, and there were no alcohol containers in the cab. When the officer handed him a ticket, the man held it at arm's length, squinting. Then, he sighed and took off his glasses.

7: Deception

A banner floated across the intersection.

Free: Hopes and Dreams. Hurry, fading fast. Vote Communist.

"That sounds like just what we need."

"It's about time someone turned this country around."

"What could possibly be wrong with that?"

8: An Outlier

You have probably seen the T-shirts and bumper stickers. The redwoods of Arizona are spectacular. Each year, thousands of tourists seek out the cluster of sixty-four redwoods soaring 250-300 feet toward the desert sun. For nearly 1500 years, they have survived the desert climate near the Colorado River on the western Arizona border.

Approached from either the Sonoran Desert to the east or the Mojave Desert to the west, the trees present a majestic landmark. It is a forested oasis, with the adjacent Colorado River providing the essential source of water. The nearby hot springs are renowned for their healing properties.

The area, originally inhabited by the Mojave people, proved popular with the Spaniards, trappers, and pioneers. In the mid-twentieth century, Parker Dam created Lake Havasu to the north. Now the redwoods are part of Cattail Cove State Park.

In the early twentieth century, scientists were fascinated that redwoods could exist outside their natural habitat of abundant rainfall and moderate coastal temperatures. Initially, the redwoods were mistaken for a variant of the giant sequoias that grow at the higher elevations of Flagstaff or Prescott. However, examination and testing proved that the theory was wrong. These were actual coastal redwoods that had somehow adapted to a harsher climate. Interestingly, the trees had created their own microclimate with lower temperatures, richer soil, conserved groundwater, and captured carbon dioxide.

How the redwoods got to Arizona is a matter of much speculation. They are old enough that it is doubtful that they were introduced by man. Therefore, the initial pine cones would most likely have been transported by an animal or bird. Due to the size of the cones and the distance from the nearest Pacific Coast source, this was an exceedingly difficult task. Once the cone was dropped at the location by the Colorado River, temperature and moisture conditions would have had to be favorable for the intricate process of germination. Then the seedling would have had to thrive and reproduce additional trees. The statistical probability of all these events occurring naturally is mind-boggling. After all, redwood trees grow nowhere else but along the coasts of California and Oregon.

Is it any wonder why people flock to observe this incredible natural phenomenon?

Or so the tale goes. Unfortunately, it is all a hoax. There are indeed giant sequoias in Arizona, but no coastal redwoods. Throw in a little history and pseudoscience, and the story becomes almost believable.

Arizona is an incredible place to explore. Lake Havasu and Cattail Cove State Park are worth a visit. Just don't go looking for the redwoods of Arizona.

9: A Reckoning

An elderly couple approached the Vietnam Wall. They stood silently, reading the names etched in the black granite. Several people moved past them as they lingered by the first panel. The wife gently pushed her husband to move along more quickly, but he resisted. He reached out and touched his reflection in the stone. Then she noticed tears streaming down his cheek.

"Did you see a name you recognized?" she asked.

He shook his head, now lightly sobbing.

"You didn't serve, and I don't think you knew anyone who died over there. So why are you so emotional about this?"

His voice quivered, "These guys were all my generation. I lived the life they never had, and I feel guilty that I didn't make more of it."

"I understand how you could look at it that way, but you've lived a good life. You have nothing to be ashamed of."

His gaze remained on the names. "It's all the little things I never appreciated. The scent of a freshly cut lawn, a juicy hamburger sizzling on the grill, the perfume you spray on your neck, or the rhythmic breaths of our kids sleeping in their beds. The overlooked details that make bad days into good ones."

"I was too busy with unimportant things. I could have been a more attentive husband or father. I got to have the love and family they never did, and I took it for granted."

"That's not true, you were a good husband, a great father, and a wonderful grandfather."

"You don't understand," he said slowly. "I trivialized the life I was given. A life they sacrificed. A life any one of them could have lived better."

She put her arm around his waist and gave a gentle squeeze. Nothing more was said. She did understand, even if she didn't agree. The shared experience had changed them both.

10: Alone

Bill and Suzy sat serenely in comfortable lounge chairs on their deck, looking out at another gorgeous sunset over the Pacific. Each held a crystal tumbler of gin and tonic with a large, round cube of ice. The evening cocktail had been a ritual since the first year of their marriage, nearly sixty years ago. They had worked hard to enjoy quiet moments of luxury like this.

The golden couple had met in high school. Even then, it was clear they were destined for great things. After graduation, they left Indiana for the glamour of Los Angeles. As each slowly worked their way up to responsible executive positions, financial security and then prosperity followed. Their modest first home was replaced by a succession of larger homes in more prestigious neighborhoods.

Their social circle changed with each new move. Gradually, only a few truly good friends remained, loyal souls willing to tolerate the never-ending quest for bigger and better. Two or three couples who could be depended upon for the celebration of special occasions or holidays.

Bill and Suzy had postponed starting a family, waiting until they could afford to give their children the very best. They dreamed of private schools, international travel, and a beautiful home. But sometime in their forties, they realized they might never be able to provide all they had imagined. By then, nature had quietly closed that door. Adoption of an infant was no longer a realistic option, and they didn't feel prepared to raise an older child.

Instead, they chose to pour their love into their nieces and nephews and the children of close friends. They convinced themselves it was a win-win, all the joy and none of the long-term responsibility or expense.

Their financial success and personal freedom allowed them to travel extensively. They visited every continent and virtually every accessible country. The stories of their adventures were the envy of their friends and family.

Over time, their friends passed away or moved closer to their children. Siblings were also gone, and the nieces and nephews were now busy with careers and families of their own.

Now nearly eighty, they looked back on full, rich lives. Suzy glanced over at Bill and realized that he was all she had, but truthfully, they had always been *alone* since the move to California. She reached over and put her hand on his.

"Suzy, we ought to enjoy this view with our evening cocktail," Bill said sweetly.

"Honey, you have your drink in your hand," she patiently reminded him.

"Oh, right, but my ice has melted."

"Stay right there, I'll get you another ice cube." She said, gently taking his glass and heading for the kitchen.

Bill got up and followed a few steps behind, "Going in already, sweetheart?" He asked.

Tears welled up in her eyes. How could she face this—alone?

11: The Man

The students shifted in their chairs. A stoop-shouldered, elderly man shuffled to the microphone stand, a moth-eaten stuffed parrot perched on his shoulder. Barely able to raise his head to make eye contact, he began to speak in a crackling, high-pitched voice.

"Many of you don't know me; I am Samuel Sickles. Principal here at Charles Garwin Memorial High School, where we proudly bear the name of the great naturalist and evolutionary theorist.

"I want to welcome you to another exciting year in your noble quest to slightly exceed mediocrity. Rest assured that the faculty and staff are ready to empower your progress in any way possible between the hours of 8:00 a.m. and 3:15 p.m. All that we ask is that you show up and try to stay awake.

"There are a few rules that I need to go over.

1. Flash photography in the locker rooms or the teacher's lounge is prohibited.

2. Any in-person contact by parents or legal guardians with faculty or staff is strictly prohibited and will result in suspension of the parent or guardian for the remainder of the year.

3.   *Optional Attendance Mondays* are optional for the teachers and staff only; student attendance is still mandatory.

"A wide range of extracurricular activities is available, and I encourage you to attend and support these. Obviously, participation in these activities has been predetermined by the coaches and staff based on your performance in middle school. Please respect this tradition.

"In addition, we are proud to have guidance counselors and an adequately trained nurse available. Please feel free to avail yourselves of their services, but be realistic in your expectations. You can only expect to go so far…and live so long.

"I nearly forgot to mention that a parole officer is available on the first Wednesday of each month for your convenience.

"Before I dismiss you to go to your homerooms, are there any questions?"

A bookish-looking boy in the front row asked, "What's with the parrot?"

"What parrot?" the principal replied with a confused look.

The long-dead parrot winked.

12: The Little Things

At first, it was just a numbness in Andy's hands and feet. A strong, gregarious man, he had thrived on strenuous manual labor and tried to work through it. But his body was beginning to betray him. In time, fatigue and shortness of breath forced him to give up working at the job site. He transitioned to using his experience to estimate and bid jobs. He was excellent at this, but a progressive tremor compounded the numbness in his hands. Eventually, he was unable even to use a calculator or keyboard.

It felt like admitting defeat to apply for disability, but he had a family to support. He struggled with his pride and adjusted. During the required physical evaluation, bladder cancer was diagnosed. He had just begun treatment when he was found to have Hodgkin's lymphoma. His condition slowly deteriorated to absolute misery. Doctors tried myriad treatments without improvement. Andy finally refused further intervention and surrendered to his fate.

In the end, he was bitter and almost impossible to be around. It broke the hearts of his wife, Jane, and their two grown children. This was not the man they knew or wanted to remember.

Andy's illness and death reduced Jane to a quietly depressed soul, just going through the motions of life. She found escape in her work and continued teaching at the local high school. But her income was modest. She struggled, but like her husband, her pride kept her from seeking assistance.

An offhand comment during a visit to her gynecologist revealed her situation. The doctor paused. He hadn't known Andy, so he asked about his illness. He suspected the symptoms might be related to Andy's service in Vietnam, and he put Jane in touch with the Veterans Affairs office.

Several months later, the doctor received a handwritten letter from Jane. She was now receiving a monthly benefit as a result of her husband's exposure to Agent Orange. She profusely thanked the doctor. She continued to work, but now had a little extra at the end of each month—something she never dreamed she would have. It was validation that Andy's sacrifice and suffering hadn't been in vain.

After nearly forty years of practice, that letter remains one of the physician's most prized possessions—acknowledgement of a small gesture that made a life-changing impact on the widow of a fellow veteran.

13: The Vacation

Jessie was seven in the summer of 1958, and his parents were planning a vacation. His dad had two weeks off from work, and they were going to load up the car and head for the Black Hills. To be honest, Jessie was not all that wild about the idea. Understandably, he and his older sister had tried to convince their parents that California was a much better vacation spot. They lost that discussion.

Their parents were firm. "We're driving to South Dakota. You're lucky to get a vacation, and it'll be fun."

Jessie, Jennie, their mom, and dad piled into their 1956 Dodge Coronet and headed for Rapid City. Their first stop was in Sioux Falls to visit Aunt Letie. She insisted that they see Devil's Gulch, where Jesse James leaped a canyon on horseback while being chased by a posse. Jessie was intrigued. He thought it was very cool.

Then the family followed the numerous highway signs to Wall Drug. It may have been interesting to the parents, but it wasn't nearly as neat as Devil's Gulch, at least to Jessie.

After that, the road took them west toward Mitchell, where their mom and dad had another must-see in mind, the Corn Palace. It was a castle covered in colored corn. Jennie thought it was pretty. Mom marveled at the artistry. Dad wondered about rats. Jessie was just bored.

They had rented a cabin on Sylvan Lake, with easy access to all the tourist spots in the Rapid City area. Jessie loved the cabin and the lake; it was so much fun.

The first trip was, of course, to Mount Rushmore. Jessie squinted at the faces from the patio of the visitor center. He was not impressed. It was supposed to be huge, but it just didn't look that big. He did learn a lot about the Presidents, though.

By far, the best part of the trip for Jessie was Deadwood. They went into the saloon where Wild Bill Hickok was actually shot and visited Boot Hill—even cooler than Devil's Gulch. Jessie and Jennie even had a sarsaparilla at the bar.

They spent a morning at Trout Haven catching rainbow trout, which they had for lunch.

At Dinosaur Park, Jessie and Jennie climbed up onto life-sized cement dinosaurs. They had their pictures taken with giant tortoises and alligators at Reptile Gardens.

Everyone enjoyed the time at the lake. Exploring and hiking were great. Jessie did not want to leave, but it was a long two-day drive home. Mom and Dad had been right. He was lucky to get a vacation, and it was fun. He could hardly wait for school to start so he could tell his friends. They'd all be jealous of his picture by Wild Bill's grave.

In his mind, Jessie was already making plans for the next family vacation. Maybe this time, he'd win the argument for California.

14: Grand Jury

The frail woman in her late fifties slipped her key into the front door lock. The only thought on her mind was sitting down for the first time in eighteen hours over a plate of warmed-up meatloaf and a cold beer. She worked two jobs during the week and another on Saturdays. Her evening meal was the highlight of her day.

She opened the door to the pungent odor of weed. Her thirty-something son and late-twentyish daughter reclined stoned on the living room couch. Beer cans, empty Frito bags, and other unidentifiable trash littered the floor. The monotonous background sounds of a video game blared from the TV. They did not acknowledge her as she moved past to the kitchen.

She opened the refrigerator and nearly cried as she realized her prized leftovers were gone. Actually, everything, except for a few condiments, was gone.

"What happened to my meatloaf?" She asked, hoping against hope that somehow it had survived.

"We were hungry," came the reply from no one in particular.

"Very considerate, what am I supposed to eat?" She said with the first hint of anger.

"You should have stopped on the way home for groceries. You're the one with all the money." The son shot back.

Now falling into a familiar pattern, she let her frustration out. "Listen, you and your sister are perfectly capable of finding jobs and contributing something around here. Why am I supporting adult children whose only ambition is to get high and play video games?"

As she said this, she stepped back into the kitchen.

The daughter replied in a slow, slurred voice. "Get off our backs, you're lucky to have us here to look after things while you're gone all day long."

"Gone all day, gone all day. You ungrateful little parasites." Just then, she spotted the knife block on the kitchen counter and instinctively reached for a carving fork.

Brandishing the fork, she charged into the living room. She knew she might regret it later, but she was at her wits' end. "Get out, get the Hell out of my house!"

Genuinely shocked, the son and daughter fled to their rooms and locked the doors.

"I said, get out of my house!" She screamed, pounding on their doors.

The daughter dialed 911. "Help, she's attacking us," a panic-laced voice cried into the phone.

****

The grand jury took less than five minutes to refuse to return an indictment in the case.

The consensus was summed up by the statement of one juror, "Personally, I would have grabbed something other than the carving fork."

15: Confusion

The man in dark slacks, a T-shirt, and a ski mask peered in through the window. He viewed five well-dressed women adorned in expensive jewelry, sipping wine, and talking enthusiastically. He circled the house looking for any sign of additional inhabitants. Finding no one else, he entered through the unlocked front door.

"Pardon me, may I help you?" asked one of the ladies in a particularly bold manner.

The man produced a gun and a pillowcase. "All your jewelry and the contents of your purses into the bag. NOW!"

"Excuse me?" one of the ladies replied.

"Don't mess with me! I said, put it all in the bag—NOW!"

"Are you robbing us? I don't understand. Why are you doing this?" another woman exclaimed.

"Seriously, we vote for all the right people; we supported 'Defund the Police' and progressive prosecutors," the bold one responded in a condescending tone.

"Lady, what are you talking about? Everything in the bag!" the thief responded incredulously.

"Let me just write you a check. How much would be enough to compensate you for your inconvenience?" asked a rather plump lady, well-versed in negotiations.

A shot fired into the ceiling elicited screams and immediate compliance with the demands for jewelry and purse contents. The thief exited calmly through the front door.

"Well, that was rude!" someone said.

"Absolutely, after all the support we've given people like him. I can't believe he would behave in that manner," the plump one added.

"Should we call the police?" asked a timid voice.

"Obviously, that poor man has been the victim of some horrible injustice. I would hate to see him traumatized any further," came a strong voice from the couch.

"The police would only make things worse by casting us as the victims and punishing that poor soul for his desperation. I can't see how anything good would come from involving the police," a confident voice offered.

"Agreed," three said in unison.

Guardedly, the timid one asked, "But… what if he robs someone else?"

16: The Counselor

Leon and Tamara were called into the office. Dr. Jampolsky sat in a stuffed chair, a notepad on his lap, and a laptop open on a small table to his left. A couch sat across from the doctor, flanked by a stuffed chair on either side. The couple sat together on the sofa.

"What brings you in today?" the doctor asked, making eye contact with each of them.

Tamara began, "Our friends staged an intervention and recommended…"

"Demanded would be more accurate," Leon interjected.

"…*suggested*…that we see you. They were disturbed that we're nearly at our tenth anniversary and still quite compatible. All of them are on at least their second marriage at this point. They see no toxicity in our relationship."

"I understand," the doctor replied. "The services of a divorce counselor are something most couples don't realize they need without the intercession of concerned family or friends."

He picked up his computer and swiped the screen. "I have reviewed the conflict and annoyance survey you completed, and I can understand your friends' concerns. Your tolerance of your partner's flaws and willingness to adapt are major red flags. Left unchecked, this sort of behavior can lead to decades of emotional stability."

"I do wish Leon were more helpful with the cooking and clean up, but he does so much with the yard, repairs, and bill paying that I don't make a big deal of it."

"Leon, how do you feel about what Tamara just said?" the doctor asked.

"We help each other out, but there are things she's better at and vice versa. It works for us."

"Exactly! This is an excellent area for conflict, and you two are not taking advantage of it. Divorce doesn't just happen; you have to work at it. You can't relax in a marriage."

"That may be what our friends are noticing. They do seem to be tense and upset with each other most of the time." Tamara acknowledged.

"I must warn you; I've seen many couples like you that compromise themselves into thirty, forty, even fifty years of marriage. You wouldn't keep the same car for that long—tires need replacing, the paint fades, Bluetooth stops syncing. It's only natural to move on every few years to a new and improved model."

"Actually, my old car was much better than the new one," Leon interrupted.

"We need to work on your positivity, Leon, but that's all the time we have for today. Let me set you up to return next week to go into some of these issues further."

"Ah… we'll need to get back to you on that," they replied together.

17: The Reunion

Animosity is a hardy plant that thrives with minimal cultivation. Even when seemingly eradicated, it can spring back to life from the tiniest residual root. We are never truly free of it.

Once a year, the tribes travel from the East and West for a unity gathering. Safe travel across borders is guaranteed for the event. For one day, all hostility is set aside and harmony prevails.

Brothers hug brothers, children play with their cousins, and leaders laugh and share stories of the old times. Food and drink are shared in abundance. Competitions among individuals and tribes celebrate their common history.

It is a great honor to be chosen to host the event—an opportunity to showcase the host tribe's accomplishments and culture. Pride is taken in ensuring that everyone feels welcome. In return, guest tribes extend warmth and praise to the host. Paramount is the code that some things are never said.

For one day, a tiny utopia exists. Things are as they were in the beginning—and as they should be again.

Then, the sun sets. The tribes gather their people and depart. As they travel to their homelands, under the protection of safe passage, old grievances are remembered. Friendship and cooperation fade.

Animosity springs from its old roots.

We wonder, what have we become? Or perhaps, we were always like this.

18: The Watch

I was born in New York City in the summer of 1949—a Bulova His Excellency XX men's wristwatch. I was designed to be elegant, yet unassuming. My 21-jewel movement was encased in 14K gold and fitted with a brown alligator leather band. From the factory floor, I traveled by train to Panke Jewelry in Manly, Nebraska.

The first week of December, I was removed from the display case and examined by a wrinkled woman in her mid-sixties. This would turn out to be Anita Spencer, the second wife of a retired farmer. She was looking for a Christmas present for her husband, Henry. She thought he needed a replacement for the nickel-plated pocket watch he had carried for decades. My design was just the right blend of stylish simplicity, and at $49.50, I was priced well within her budget.

Henry and Anita were an odd couple. Henry had lost his wife a couple of years before and hired Anita as a housekeeper and cook. They proved to be compatible and decided to marry. There was little romance. Henry brought the checkbook, and Anita provided everything else. The situation seemed to work, or at least they were satisfied with the arrangement.

I was a pleasant surprise for Henry. He seemed genuinely pleased and immediately strapped me to his wrist. I spent most of the next ten years there. Henry took excellent care of me, avoiding any potentially harmful situations. Routine cleanings and maintenance were carefully performed. Then Henry lay down one night and died.

Henry had a son, Carlton, and Anita passed me on to him. Carlton was much more active than Henry, and I spent most of my time in a drawer. Only for special occasions did Carlton take me out, wind me, and put me on. Those were my quiet years.

Everything changed when Carlton got sick. He began wearing me all the time. These were great times for me, but not for Carlton. It didn't escape me that the last time I was regularly worn was when Henry's time was winding down. In time, like his father, Carlton grew weak and eventually died.

After Carlton's funeral, his wife pulled their oldest son, Chip, aside.

"Chip, this was your grandfather's watch. He was wearing it *when he died*. Your father was wearing it *when he died*. Now I want you to have it," she said, unaware of the implication.

Chip's brother asked him what their mom had said to him.

"She said she wants *you* to have grandpa's watch," Chip told his brother.

I noticed Chip's hand trembling as he passed me to his brother.

19: Communication

Jane and her mother sat across from each other at a small table in the Olive Garden, eagerly munching on their salads.

"Mom, there's something I need to talk to you about. I know you've been extremely proud of Katherine…"

"Sister Mary Agnes."

"Mom, Katherine has decided to leave the convent…"

"Why on earth would she leave the convent? She's always been so devout. We need to get her into counseling, get things straightened out…"

"Mom, she's already seen the Archdiocese counselors. It's her decision. What she needs now is our support. This is tough for her."

"At least tell me why she would do this. Is she going through a crisis of Faith?"

"No, Mom, nothing like that. She feels her true calling is to be a thespian. She wants to pursue that."

"Well, Jane, I'm not sure that qualifies as a 'calling'. I think the kids nowadays think of it more as an identification or lifestyle choice."

Jane's mom hesitates for a moment, pondering whether to share, then continues, almost whispering.

"I know it may come as a shock to you, but I have always suspected that many of the nuns were of that persuasion. When I was in school, we all thought that Sister Bernadette and Sister Margaret Catherine had a thing for each other."

"No, no, not lesbian, thespian—an actor."

"PotAto, potahto, they're all the same."

"No, Mom, she wants to act in plays. She wants to study acting."

"Oh. Well, that's the highway to Hell if you ask me! But, of course, I'll support Sister, er…Katherine, in whatever ridiculous thing she does. I just hope she comes to her senses before I die. That's all I ask."

"Thanks, Mom, I knew you'd understand. How's your salad?"

"You know I love the endless salad and breadsticks. We should do this more often."

20: An Omen

Florence had met the perfect man and was deeply in love. Nearly five years had passed since Roger's death, and she was finally ready to move on. Andy was handsome, attentive, and financially secure. A life together promised to be relaxed and exciting. Their wedding was only a week away.

Then Roger appeared, at least a specter that looked just like him, warning her not to marry Andy. At first, she thought it was only a bad dream—perhaps "survivor's" guilt or something like that. However, Roger was persistent. He appeared whenever Florence was alone. Always repeating the same warning that she would regret marrying Andy. She tried to interact with the apparition, but Roger would offer nothing more than the ambiguous warning.

She thought about confiding in her friends but hesitated. They all thought Andy was wonderful, and she just knew they would tell her she was having last-minute "jitters."

As she stood one last time—gazing at her wedding dress, hair, and makeup—Roger appeared in the mirror behind her. He stood there silent, only a sad look on his face.

The wedding was beautiful, perfect in fact. They honeymooned in Turks and Caicos and settled into their newlywed life. They shared everything and seemed completely compatible.

Andy included Florence in his business decisions. He'd bring her morning coffee and spreadsheets. She found his import/export business fascinating. He gave her a 20% share in the business and the title of executive consultant. Her background was in real estate, and she began to advise him on property investments in the Caribbean. Andy even titled the property in St. Barts in her name. Life was good. Andy was everything she had hoped for—and more. The ghost of Roger was completely forgotten.

Florence planned a girls' trip to St. Barts with her friends. They were lounging by the pool when the police arrived. To her horror and humiliation, the police had a warrant for her arrest. She was charged with money laundering. The money she had helped Andy invest in Caribbean properties came from an array of illicit activities. Her official role in the business, along with the villa in St. Barts registered solely in her name, was a devastating liability.

Her calls to Andy went unanswered. He had vanished without a trace. Her assets were frozen. Her lawyer was not encouraging.

Roger would never appear to Florence again, but in the cold silence of sleepless nights, his warning echoed in her ears.

21: Confirmation

The Senate hearing on the nomination of Clearmont Hemmings had progressed to its second witness. The Chairman recognized the senior Senator from Louisiana.

Senator Hruba began in a slow, almost theatrical, southern drawl, "In the interest of full disclosure, I must begin with a statement. I am proud to say that my friendship with Judge Hemmings dates back several decades to when we were classmates at LSU. I had the distinct privilege of nominating him to the state bench during my time as Governor of our great state. I know him to be an outstanding jurist and a brilliant legal scholar."

Turning to the witness, he continued. "Judge Leonard, you've served for several years on the Court of Appeals with Judge Hemmings, is that correct?"

"Yes, Senator, I believe it's been seven years."

"Then would you agree with my assessment that Judge Hemmings is an outstanding jurist and a brilliant legal scholar?"

"Respectfully, Senator, those are not the words I would have chosen."

"Fine, fine, in your own words then, how would you describe the nominee?"

Judge Leonard paused, then shrugged slightly. "Eh, 'mediocre' most honestly describes my assessment."

Senator Hruba perked up. "Excellent, I can work with that. Our fine country is primarily populated by people who could truthfully be described as mediocre. Heh, heh… There are even those in some circles who would describe *me* as mediocre. Wouldn't you agree, Judge, that all those mediocre people deserve representation on the United States Supreme Court by a mediocre justice?"

"Absolutely, Senator, I wholeheartedly agree that there are many people who would consider you mediocre."

"Now, Mr. Leonard, that is not what I was asking, is it?" The Senator responded with a kind smile.

"I'm sorry, Senator, I was just agreeing with your statement."

Senator Hruba turned to the Chairman and partially covered his microphone, "It appears that this dog has crawled under the porch. No further questions for the witness, Mr. Chairman."

22: The Image

It was a scene repeated in countless other places and at countless other times. A father and mother prepared to bid their loved one goodbye on the way to war. The mother attempted small talk, barely holding back tears. The father was silent, his fear poorly hidden. He knew what his son was about to encounter. The young soldier was lost in thought and barely aware of what was happening around him.

The train pulled in, and it was time to board. The soldier stood, grabbed his duffle, and turned to his parents. Tears streamed down his mother's face, her body heaving with sobs as she engulfed the young man in a bear hug, not wanting to let go.

The father gently separated his wife and son. The son timidly asked his father if he had any last advice.

"Just do as you're told, own up to your mistakes, and always tell the truth," Was the reply.

"I thought you were going to say, 'Keep your head down,'" the boy said, somewhat surprised.

"That's not always going to be possible," his father thought, but wisely did not say.

The soldier held out his hand to his father, who grabbed it and pulled him in for a heartfelt hug. Then he turned and boarded the train.

There were a dozen pictures of their soldier son throughout their home, but the memory of him boarding that train was the image they held in their hearts.

23: The Christmas Spirit

Though the details have faded with time, the heart of this memory, etched in my seven-year-old mind, remains clear. Grandma and Grandpa had planned a special surprise. They had purchased a permit that allowed us to go up into the mountains to cut a live Christmas tree.

Bundled up in our heaviest winter clothes, we loaded into their car for the trip. Grandma had packed snacks and cocoa in a thermos. It took a long time to get up the mountain, but Grandma entertained me with stories, and we sang Christmas carols.

Eventually, we reached our destination. I couldn't wait to get out, but the snow surprised me—it came nearly up to the crotch of my snow pants. Grandpa grabbed a saucer sled out of the trunk and pulled me along, or else I wouldn't have been able to walk in the deep snow.

We headed up from the parking spot until I spotted the perfect tree. Grandpa began to saw it down, but he got tired and Grandma took over for a while. After a lot of effort, the tree came down.

Grandma pulled me downhill on the sled, and Grandpa dragged the tree, huffing and puffing all the way. When we got to the car, Grandpa let out a string of words that Grandma usually spelled out instead of saying. The tree was three or four feet longer than our car.

I sat in the car and warmed up as Grandpa, muttering under his breath, took the saw and cut the tree almost in half. Then it was nearly all Grandpa and Grandma could do to lift the tree onto the car roof. They tied it to the roof with twine, and we headed down the mountain.

Passing through a small town at the base of the mountain, we were back on the highway heading home. After quite a while, Grandpa pulled over to the side of the road. Something was wrong. Somehow, the tree had blown off the roof.

We began to retrace our tracks. Grandpa looked to the left while Grandma and I scanned the shoulder and ditch on the right. We saw no sign of our tree. Then we came to the small town at the base of the mountain. There, we spotted a pickup parked at a gas station with a tree in the back—that looked a lot like our tree.

As Grandpa got out and looked at the tree, a man approached the pickup.

Grandpa asked, "Did you find that tree along the side of the road?"

"Maybe," the man smirked. "What's it worth to you?"

"Buddy, you have no idea."

24: The Sacrifice

After two long days of cleaning out her mother's house, Maura was exhausted. She had spent hours sifting through drawers and closets, each with mysterious treasures. She wasn't sentimental, but tossing all this away felt like erasing people she never really knew.

Her father had died five years ago, and she should have offered to help her mother sort things out then. She had been adopted late in their lives and had no idea of the history or significance of much of what she was now encountering.

Regardless, it was her job now, but she needed a break. She found an odd tea bag in the cupboard and brewed a large cup. Nestled onto the couch, wrapped in a comfy Afghan, tea in hand, she flipped on the TV and began to channel surf. A hokey sci-fi mystery popped up. Mindless drivel was just what she needed.

The lead actor and actress seemed vaguely familiar. It was a story of blossoming love set during the summer of 1974, full of the naiveté of youth. The guy was quite attractive, and the girl was quirky and engaging. The background music of the Eagles, Beach Boys, and Moody Blues flowed easily into her ears. The couple met a mysterious old woman, who passed on a potion to ensure their love would live on forever. After their death, a sacrifice would be required to guarantee their resurrection and immortality.

She awoke, surprised to realize that she had dozed off. That tea had packed quite a punch. She felt not quite herself. A shiver ran down her spine as she detected the actor from the movie sitting on the couch beside her. She jumped up and ran to the bathroom and locked the door.

Then she caught a glimpse of herself in the bathroom mirror. Only the image was that of the actress from the movie. What the…

"Babe, you OK in there? I can't believe we did it, really did it!" It was her father's voice.

Then it hit her. She recognized the actors in the movie as her adoptive parents from old photos she had seen. What had they done?

Was this a dream, a nightmare? Was she hallucinating? What was in that tea?

A knock at the bathroom door, "Come on out, let me give you a hug. I know it's a little unsettling, but we planned this for so many years. I still can't believe it actually worked!"

Maura was still Maura, but she looked like a younger version of her mother. Clearly, it hadn't worked the way they had planned. How was she going to deal with her suddenly undead father? How was she going to explain her new "look" to her own husband? And most importantly, why had they done this to her?

Tentatively, she opened the door and crossed the threshold. Suddenly, Maura ceased to exist.

25: The Lover

The warm summer sun peeked down through scattered cumulus clouds onto a lonely patch of I-10 in southwest Texas. He spotted an old friend, Jodi, driving a Wild Cherry Chevy Camaro convertible. A flicker of joy passed through him. He didn't often play favorites, but he'd always made an exception for Jodi. She had loved him from an early age, loved him openly—and he, in turn, had never looked away.

She was a gorgeous California girl. He had caressed her skin with his rays for decades. She maintained a beautiful golden tan at age forty-two, with just a hint of the attractive wrinkles and dryness that he offered all his devotees. Her strawberry blonde hair displayed the sun-bleached accents he preferred.

He had always appreciated her athleticism. She loved his favorite sports: beach volleyball, rollerblading, surfing, golf, and jogging. This afforded them more time together. She never shielded herself from his health-giving rays with sunscreen. He returned the favor with abundant vitamin D.

Jodi took a sip of Diet Coke.

Oh, Jodi, he thought. *Don't do that. That aspartame can kill you.*

She was a confident, independent woman—an attorney unimpeded by the anchor of a man. Her bronzed beauty, a gift from him, had allowed her to love if and when she wanted. The sun had taken great pleasure in following her through the years, making himself available whenever she needed him.

Jodi leaned forward to adjust the visor. A spot with variable pigmentation and irregular borders was visible on the back of her right shoulder. The sun immediately recognized a melanoma. He had been through this too many times before. He knew his time with Jodi would soon be over. It saddened him—girls like Jodi were hard to find in the current age of sunblock, hats, and swim covers.

Soon, the medical naysayers would be driving a wedge between them. He took comfort in the knowledge that it was not his fault. Without his warm, life-giving rays, the Earth would be a cold, dark rock.

Jodi had known the risks. Skin cancer was a small price to pay for all he had given her.

26: Arrogance

The Headquarters building was a long, rectangular white clapboard structure with a wide veranda supported on brick pillars. A sergeant sat at a small desk in the outer room, glancing up from a dog-eared ledger. A Currier and Ives calendar hung on the wall, flipped to November 1914. Without a word, he motioned the Lieutenant inside.

The Lieutenant approached the Colonel's desk, came to attention, stated his name and rank, and sharply saluted.

The Colonel came straight to the point. "Lieutenant, you have disqualified twenty percent of the prospective trainees in the aviation section. That is unacceptable. I expect you to review your recommendations and reduce that number to no more than five percent."

"Sir, as a physician, I cannot ignore obvious physical—"

The Lieutenant stopped mid-sentence when the Colonel rapped his Academy ring sharply on his desk, like a gavel. A clear signal among Old Grads.

"You are a First Lieutenant in the United States Army Medical Corps," he snapped. "I expect you to act like an officer and consider the mission first. These men aren't fit for the Cavalry or the Infantry.

They have been assigned to the Signal Corps specifically to train as pilots in this new aviation section…and **that** is what they are going to do! Am I clear?"

"Sir, may I ask…is it not my responsibility to make certain that valuable government personnel and equipment are not needlessly endangered?"

"I don't know of a G*d* Lieutenant in the Army—**especially** in the Medical Corps—who is expected to think for himself. You are presuming to question my orders!"

He leaned back, voice laced with sarcasm, "But just to make certain you understand, these idiotic flying kites are a passing fancy. They may have some minor value for observation, but are worthless as offensive weapons."

He sneered, "**Real men** fight face to face, seeing each other through iron sights or down the blade of a saber. Did that Ivy League medical school erase everything you learned at the Academy?"

Leaning in, his eyes narrowed, "These flyers are just fancy boys seeking suicidal adventure. I will not stand in their way. And **neither will you!**"

"Sir…"

"You are dismissed, Lieutenant!"

The Lieutenant stiffened to attention, smartly saluted, did a sharp about-face, and exited.

He drew strength from the lessons learned at West Point. As an officer and a physician, he had sworn distinct oaths—and he would honor both. He would find another way.

27: An Ending

William Penn, M.D., wandered the grocery parking lot squinting against the sun for a white mid-sized sedan lost among a sea of nearly identical cars. It wasn't the first time he had forgotten where he parked, and the frustration and embarrassment grew with each recurrence.

Things had not always been like this. The doctor had once been the backbone of the community. When the other doctors in town had been drafted and gone off to war, the senior physician remained behind and filled the void. He was the only one there for the colds, injuries, deliveries, and major illnesses. He performed countless appendectomies, gallbladders, and c-sections. In a time when world events were often grim, Dr. Penn was a soft voice and a steady, comforting hand in their small town.

Now, his kind spirit and dedication were counterbalanced by fading knowledge and skills. He had become a liability to the profession. The hospital medical staff held a private ad hoc meeting to discuss the situation. The consensus was that Dr. Penn would not willingly retire. The subject had been broached with him numerous times, always without success.

Dr. Schultz, a cynical young physician, offered an audacious solution. They would approach the newspaper with the announcement that Dr. Penn was retiring on a set date, and the medical staff would host a retirement party in his honor. The entire community would be invited to celebrate. Dr. Schultz's convoluted logic was that the move would be so bold, the public involvement so extensive, that Dr. Penn would feel compelled to "play along".

To everyone's amazement, the plan unfolded without protest. The public response exceeded all expectations, evolving into a weeklong series of tributes and presentations.

A dinner hosted by the medical staff culminated the festivities. One by one, his fellow physicians rose to offer heartfelt testimonies. The highlight came with the presentation of a "golden medical license" by the State Medical Society to Dr. Penn for his over 50 years of dedication to the profession. He beamed proudly at his name engraved on the impressive plaque. Perhaps he had done enough.

Dr. Penn lingered in the emptying room and pulled Dr. Schultz aside for a quiet word.

"I understand that you were the one behind all this. I know this was the right thing to do, but I never would have taken that step on my own. I'm proud to have been your colleague."

Tears welled in Dr. Schultz's eyes as the weight of his deception pressed against his cynical heart. He hadn't expected that.

28: Exposure

The guest was more than a little apprehensive. The *Don Harper Experience* provided excellent exposure for her message, but carried the risk of devastating ridicule. Nothing was out of bounds in his quest for ratings. She hoped to get her word out without stepping on a landmine.

Don leaned forward and warmly spoke into camera 1. "I am very pleased to welcome Pauline Dresser, Distinguished Professor of Environmental Social Sciences at Stanford University. Dr. Dresser is here to discuss her New York Times best seller, *The End of Life as We Know It*. In it, she predicts that all life on planet Earth will end in 10 years.

"So, Professor, please explain to our viewers why they are all doomed."

Pauline took a deep breath; she felt she was already in a deep hole. "Thank you, Don. First of all, I'm not predicting anything. I'm merely sharing the results of highly complex computer scenarios that indicate that there will be critical water shortages within 10 years. Those shortages may lead to life extinction events."

"In other words, we are going to run out of water and are all doomed."

"Don, there are large populations in arid regions that are already facing critical water shortages. The diminishing rainfall associated with progressive climate change, coupled with expanded use of fresh water resources for non-agricultural irrigation, manufacturing, and industrial purposes, will ultimately result in a global water shortage. Crops will fail, disease will spread, and finally life may no longer be sustainable."

"OK, that's certainly encouraging, Professor," Don said with a sarcastic grin. "I'm sure you have a bold, progressive, environmentally intrusive plan to save us all. Tell us what we need to do."

Pauline immediately recognized his ploy. "The purpose of my book is to inform, to allow everyone to have the same information I have. I'm sorry to say that I don't have a solution. Our computer analysis does not reveal any effective means to reverse current trends. The title, *The End of Life as We Know It*, is meant to convey that all of us will be faced with life-altering, possibly threatening changes."

She continued, "The ultimate outcome will occur in 5 years at a minimum and 10 years at the most. The geographic extremes of the northern and southern hemispheres will be the first to experience extinction-level degradation. The panic and mass migration will push the rapidly worsening crisis toward the more densely populated central latitudes. Europe and the United States will be the last to succumb."

"So, as I've stated twice now, we are all doomed." Don leaned in for the kill shot. "Professor, you've clearly stated your disbelief in God in your book and previous interviews. Let me ask you this: What is keeping you from living like there is no tomorrow? I mean, if you don't believe in an afterlife, then there are no consequences for your actions. The world is going to end before you can be brought to justice here. What is keeping you from raping, pillaging, and plundering—so to speak?"

Without hesitation, Pauline responded, "Mr. Harper, my morality is grounded in my love for my fellow man and not in fear of divine or legal retribution. I could no more engage in such reprehensible behavior than I could encourage others to do so."

The producer signaled Don to cut too commercial.

"We'll be right back after this word from one of our fine sponsors."

The producer's voice came through his earpiece, "Outstanding. One of your best, Don."

Don grinned widely and his eyes twinkled, "Well done, Professor—you're quite good at this! By the way, did you ever share an office with Paul Ehrlich?"

Pauline's head sank to her chest and slowly moved side to side.

The producer signaled: *Back in 5, 4, 3, 2…*

29: Irritating

Nobody liked Carney Wilson. This wasn't because he was a lawyer, although that was reason enough. He wasn't mean, or rude, or even disagreeable. He was simply annoying. The very traits that made him a successful attorney doomed him socially.

Most people agreed that Carney had no idea how irritating he was. Perhaps he should have gotten a hint when he never had a second date or an invitation to a social gathering. He could turn a five-second question into a ten-minute answer. Some people are brutally honest, but Carney was maddeningly trivial. His opinion on punctuation corrections in the Pledge of Allegiance was not of interest to anyone.

He routinely turned yes or no situations into monologues. There is absolutely no need to know a detailed profile of groundwater contaminants when asked if you would like something to drink.

He found his true calling as a mediator in divorce cases. He had a near-perfect record at bringing opposing parties to compromise and closure in record time. They couldn't get to the door fast enough.

The contrast with his brother, Barney, was striking. Barney was gregarious, funny, and a delight to converse with. Sure, he worked in the sewers, and yes, he had a certain odor. But he was so much fun to be around that everyone was willing to overlook a minor occupational consequence. He never lacked for company or sandalwood-scented gift baskets.

After nearly forty-five years and over two thousand fractured marriages mediated, Carney decided to retire. The local Bar Association wanted to recognize his significant contribution to the profession, but they were also well aware that he was a social pariah. They hit upon the perfect solution: they would arrange for Barney to host a roast in his brother's honor.

Not surprisingly, there was a huge public response. It's fair to say that the majority of those in attendance had last been in the same room with Carney when he mediated their divorce. However, the opportunity to spend an evening with Barney was enough to bring them together again.

A splendid dinner was served. Local Bar officials presented Carney with a plaque and said some very complimentary things. Then Barney rose to speak—grinning, of course.

"Many times, I've been told that my brother and I are very different. That just isn't so. For instance, we both have a mysterious ability to turn your stomach…"

30: Echoes

About a dozen fifth and sixth-graders gathered around the still-smoking remains of their school, the air thick with the scent of charred wood and a faint trace of asbestos. Jimmy approached and high-fived Aaron.

"Can you believe it? The weekend before the start of school, and the dump burns down! What are the odds?" He said with a broad grin and a fist pump.

"Did you hear about Roger's dad?" Aaron asked.

"No, what happened?"

"My dad said that he's the one who caused the fire," Aaron replied.

Jimmy was defiant, "No way, he's an OK dude. No way he would do this!"

"I heard it was an accident; he was working on the plumbing or something," Elsa said.

Serena chimed in, "My mom said he doesn't have insurance to cover big buildings, like a school. He could go bankrupt."

"Well, my dad said he wasn't even supposed to be working here,"

Duane explained. "He just filled in cause the regular guy's in the hospital."

"I should go find Roger. I'll bet he's feeling pretty bad," Jimmy said, his voice quieter as he looked down and kicked a clump of torn-up sod. He didn't feel like grinning anymore.

"My mom said that Roger and his mom are staying with his grandma until things settle down," Cheryl whispered as if it were a secret.

Pat added, "Yeah, my folks said that the lawyers are going to rake him over the coals."

"Well, in things like this, the lawyers are the only ones who win," Elsa said, like it was something everyone should agree with.

"Lawyers," Dean said with disgust, "They're the ones that killed Jesus, you know."

"Eh… Dean, I don't think that's true." Jimmy continued, "Maybe your dad just hates lawyers 'cause your mom got his truck in the divorce?"

"Probably…but still, Roger's dad is screwed."

"You think Roger's family will have to move away?" Jimmy asked in a shaky voice.

No one answered, the impact of the question echoing in their ears.

31: Illogic

The 1850's

"Have you heard about President Taylor?"

"No, what's he done now?"

"He died."

"What happened?"

"Apparently, he ate some cherries."

"I didn't know that was enough to kill you."

"Well, he drank some iced milk too."

"Oh, well, that explains it."

The 1960's

"President Kennedy's been shot!"

"Who did it?"

"They've caught a guy who built a sniper's nest. There are pictures of him with the gun, and he shot a police officer trying to escape."

"Sure, but there must be more to it."

The 2020's

"Trump has Covid."

"Was he vaccinated?"

"Of course! That's why he got Covid."

32: The Ugly Truth

The baby was ugly, hideous, grotesque. There was no sugar-coating it. It was difficult to look at this kid.

Yet, they had to.

With spines like Slinkies, they bent and bowed, their insincere fawning and flattery surging like sulfurous gas from a volcano.

His parents were rich and powerful. Like most, they were totally blind to the truth when it came to their own child.

He was a little prince and would be seen—and treated—as such.

The charade was delicately maintained. The young boy was sheltered from the obvious.

He had the best of everything; no desire or opportunity was denied. Praise and encouragement met his every effort.

The formula for disaster was complete.

The boy transformed into youthful adulthood. He met a young girl and fell deeply in love. He brought her home to meet his parents, who likewise recognized her beautiful soul. They saw that she truly loved their son.

With faux concern, the sycophantic entourage pulled the girl aside and told her, "You don't have to do this. We all know that you can do much better."

The girl was outraged. How could she do better? Could they not see that the young man was the sweetest, kindest, most considerate person you could ever meet?

Did they not know the boy was painfully aware of the face in the mirror and the shallowness of those around him? He had deliberately crafted his own inner beauty despite it all.

Sadly, they did not.

They had been blind—seeing only the ugliness, never the beauty.

33: The Best

Silas was very sick when he was a youngster. He spent nearly a year in the hospital. His mother was by his side, lovingly supporting him. He missed his old neighborhood and his school. He made friends with the other kids in the hospital, but there were no other black kids his age. There was no one who reminded him of home or himself.

Quite by surprise, one morning, his best friend Willie and his mother came to visit him. They had traveled all the way across the state just to cheer him up.

Willie paused when he saw Silas, without any hair and looking very skinny. But then Silas grinned, and that was all it took. He was the same Silas, still his best friend.

He started by telling Silas about everything new and exciting at school and in the neighborhood. Douglas's older brother had a go-kart. The drug store had raised the price of popsicles to ten cents. And their teacher, Miss Jones, was getting married in the summer.

Then it was Silas' turn. Willie carefully pushed him around in his wheelchair as Silas gave him a tour of the hospital. Their mothers tagged along far enough behind that the friends felt they were on their own. It was an unwitnessed kindness, one only a mother would think to give.

Willie was particularly impressed with the game room. They spent nearly two hours playing *Operation* and *Chutes and Ladders*. Willie showed no mercy, and Silas was a sore loser, as usual.

Silas "treated" Willie and his mother to "hospital food" for lunch, and Willie promised to send some real food in the mail. Unfortunately, this was overheard by the dreaded Nurse Karlie, who informed Willie about rules, diets, and a lot of other uninteresting things.

After lunch, the boys returned to the game room to watch that day's movie, *Swiss Family Robinson*. What fun it would have been to live on an island and fight pirates. They promised to make their own island clubhouse when Silas got back to the neighborhood.

Silas was getting tired, and it was time for Willie and his mother to start their long journey home. That day, Silas was not a sick kid in the hospital. He was just a kid, laughing, imagining, and living. A day with his best friend, who saw him exactly as he was. It was the best day ever.

34: Brotherhood

Once upon a time, in a land far away, there were two brothers, Hadgi and Ewot. When they came of age, they left their family home to make their own way in the world.

Ewot chose to seek fame and fortune in the great city. There he fell in with cunning men who taught him to profit from the weakness of others. Ewot learned quickly and became rich and powerful. He forgot the ways of his youth. He grew cold and arrogant, caring only for wealth and status.

Hadgi, by contrast, became a humble worker in the orchard of an old family friend. Through diligence and honesty, he rose to the position of a trusted steward. Under his care, the orchard flourished. He married a young maiden, started a family, and when the old man died, Hadgi inherited the land. As the years passed, Hadgi and his family became widely known for their generosity and kindness to the surrounding community.

In time, the brothers' mother grew gravely ill. She clutched Hadgi's hand and whispered, "Send for your brother. Let me see him once more."

Hadgi sent his oldest son to the city. Distressed, the boy returned with Ewot's reply.

"Tell my mother that I am consumed with urgent affairs, but I send these gold coins as a token of my love for her."

Upon hearing this, his mother smiled weakly. "See how well my son has done for himself," she said and died peacefully, surrounded by Hadgi and her grandchildren.

Years later, their father, now weak with age, also asked to see Ewot one last time. Again, Hadgi dispatched a messenger.

The response came. "My father taught me the nobility of labor, and I honor him by remaining steadfast in my work. I send him these gold coins as a tribute to his teachings."

"Truly, my son has not forgotten the value of daily toil," said the father, as he died cradled in Hadgi's arms.

Time passed. Ewot's health failed. His allies, sensing weakness, abandoned him. He lost his power, and his wealth was stolen. Alone and desperate, he sent word to his brother begging for his support and mercy.

Once more, Hadgi sent his beloved son to the city. Ewot received a parcel and a note.

"My lost brother, you may remain in the place you chose over your family. As a token of my love, I send this fruit basket, harvested from the life you abandoned."

35: Unsolicited Advice

The Twilight Show host looked up from his desk, holding his nightly commentary, and began to speak in a confident voice.

"It has been said many times by many different people, 'Life is cold and hard, then you die.'"

"The wording may vary, but the message remains the same. None of us has an easy time of it. But is it true?"

"Certainly, the vast majority of humans around the world live in circumstances that require their constant effort to survive. If you don't work, you don't eat—or in the parlance of the corporate world, 'You eat what you kill.'"

"What are the exceptions? Minor children, the disabled, the elderly, and the incarcerated are groups that may come to mind. These individuals, by necessity or circumstance, rely on the labor and support of others—parents, caregivers, taxpayers—which is no less valid or essential because it comes from others."

"What about the independently wealthy? Those fortunate enough to be able to walk away from work without worry. This group would include those with inherited generational wealth, business people, entrepreneurs, athletes, and those in the entertainment industry. They may still choose to work, but survival is not an issue for them. The question for them is not whether life is cold and hard, but whether they are universally content."

"I'm going out on a limb here and guessing, no. I'll go out even a little further and suggest that any discontent is largely self-inflicted. Boredom, peer or familial pressure, image, status, envy, greed, even love are all inconsequential compared with a struggle to survive."

"Yet in this upside-down world, a select few of these people are trying to influence our decisions. They exist on two different planes. First, is the 'friend' sharing a great product or service with us? The second is the 'condescending authority,' lecturing us on how to think and even how to vote. Both are insulting."

"Let me be blunt. Their wealth or success does not empower them with any authority to tell us what to think or do. We are perfectly capable of thinking and acting on our own."

"We don't begrudge their wealth or success. Just leave us alone. We have enough to do in this cold, hard world without them hassling us."

LAUGH, CRY, CRITICIZE

He ended to thunderous cheers and applause from the audience.

****

News flash: *Hollywood A-listers boycott The Twilight Show over divisive and tone-deaf commentary.*

36: The Terror

An elderly gentleman strolled down a tree-lined New Jersey sidewalk with his miniature schnauzer. Suddenly, silently, he burst into flames. The dog ran a short distance and cowered, shaking in fear. A block away, a jogger observed the blaze and called 911. A small crowd gathered mesmerized by the otherworldly spectacle.

Authorities were unable to identify either an ignition source or the presence of accelerants. Intrigued but not alarmed, they worked on the case as an isolated incident. Spontaneous human combustion was dismissed as a myth. There had to be a logical, scientific explanation.

Public concern escalated when an eight-year-old girl was consumed by fire while sitting at her second-grade desk a few days later. The teacher momentarily froze in horror as panicked students fled the school. The death of a child brought an urgency to finding answers to the source of the tragedies.

Thus far, both events had occurred in New Jersey. A week later, a newlywed couple in Virginia were struck while sleeping in their bed. Initially, it was assumed that one or both had been smoking in bed. The fire marshal noted no evidence of smoking. Rather, it appeared that the female was very rapidly consumed by the fire, and her husband was a secondary victim. This was another apparent case of spontaneous human combustion. Was there a pattern or something the victims had in common?

A dental hygienist in Illinois had just finished with a patient when she was engulfed in flames. In a single hour, a farmer collapsed in flames in California, a housewife in Minnesota screamed mid-phone call, and a bus passenger in Atlanta died before the vehicle could even stop.

Panic and paranoia spread rapidly across the country. People became apprehensive about gatherings, public transportation, and even couples sleeping together in the same bed. Reassurance from the NIH fell on deaf ears; its credibility had been shattered by the COVID experience. People could see with their own eyes what was going on, and they were scared to death.

Then the crisis reached its tipping point. A Boeing 737 suffered an onboard fire and crashed in Colorado with the loss of all aboard. No one trusted anyone else. Everyone was viewed as a ticking time bomb that could explode at any moment. The mental health crisis was universal, and teletherapy proved ineffective. Social gatherings and interpersonal relationships ceased. TV and radio broadcasts went silent. The populace was on their own for information. The travel and hospitality industry collapsed, and widespread absenteeism soon toppled the rest of the economy.

The fires touched nearly every part of the nation and expanded internationally. Most terrifying was that no one knew why. Rumors multiplied. Misinformation spread as rapidly as the flames.

The world became savage and desperate. What can you do when everyone is a threat? Even worse, you can't trust *yourself*. How do you run from the Devil within?

37: The Sound

Silence is a lie. Even in stillness, there is something—a whirling fan, an electrical hum, the wind through the trees, the ticking of a clock, or a dripping faucet. We are surrounded by sounds. It is our nature to tune them out, to ignore the interference in our perceived peace and quiet. Only alarms and sudden loud noises demand our attention; everything else, we disregard.

Those cursed with ringing in their ears or hypersensitivity to ambient noise were desperate for help. Unfortunately, they received little empathy from their "normal" companions, who were incapable of fully understanding their dilemma. Soon, the unsympathetic would come to know, fully and terrifyingly, the power of a sound.

Without warning or discernible reason, a soft buzz—like a swarm of insects—arose. It was just as clear indoors as it was outside. No earplugs or sound-dampening headphones shielded it. Constantly present, day or night, it was everywhere—throughout the globe. Every man, woman, child, and animal heard it. There was no escape.

At first, the news reports were investigative, even reassuring. Surely, there was a logical explanation, and with that, a solution.

What began as a minor annoyance soon made it difficult to concentrate. Productivity declined. Sleep became elusive, and irritability escalated. Animal attacks were common. In short order, intolerance transformed into widespread violence. Society throughout the world was breaking down. People demanded answers and action. Something, anything, had to be done to make it stop.

Political systems everywhere disintegrated. Authoritarian regimes no longer had the compliance of their subordinates. The various representative governments became dysfunctional due to their inability to focus on any practical agenda. The infrastructure of society likewise collapsed. No one had the energy or desire to perform their jobs or carry out their responsibilities.

Once it was in their heads, it became all-consuming. Nothing else mattered. It drained life of meaning. Food lost its taste. Music and art became bland. Love was replaced by annoyance.

But why? How did it start? Why could nothing be done about it?

We will never know. The world ended—not with a bang, but with a buzz.

38: A Eulogy

A high school classmate in a nice suit rises to speak.

"Jim never wanted any of this. He once told me that he didn't want a funeral—just a simple graveside committal. He didn't think anyone would show up, and for those who might, he felt bad about them having to take time off from work.

"He was odd in that he bragged about the things he had never done and stayed modest about stuff he actually had. Over the years, he accomplished a great deal.

"I don't know of a single worthy cause that he didn't contribute to—often anonymously. He realized that he had it better in life than most, but didn't want to appear showy.

"Many people in the community benefited from his services free of charge. He once said it didn't bother him at all to give his work away, but it really bugged him to be conned by a 'homeless' person on the street.

"He served in leadership positions, yet never actively sought them. He felt pretty good about doing something meaningful, but had no interest in status. Mostly, he just wanted to fit in.

"His family was an immense source of pride. His wife and children were successful in all sorts of ways, but you'd never know it from talking to him.   Typically, he told stories where they were the punchline, because he was irritated by people acting like their families were the best-looking, smartest, and most talented. Who wanted to hear that?

"Jim was good at his work, but he never claimed to be a superstar. He once said that he was the best in town on some days, the worst in town on a few days, and pretty much like everyone else the rest of the time.

"He was strangely shy in a group but quite sociable one-on-one. He loved to tell anecdotes and jokes. His best humor was in his spontaneous comments, which were quickly forgotten.

"Still, a few of his one-liners have stuck with us:

'She had the potential to be quite beautiful, but blew it.'

'He spent all day looking for a left-handed pickleball paddle.'

'Why do blind girls feel a guy's face? They have the perfect excuse to go a little lower.'

'He keeps marrying younger and younger women. I don't think the current one is even potty trained.'

'I don't fear death, but I am little worried about the actual dying part of it.'

'Save yourself the stress, buddy. Just skip the marriage. Pick a fight with some random woman and then give her your house.'

'I don't eat salads; I like to run my greens through a cow first.'

'You really can't tell the difference between tofu and the real thing… except for the gagging part.'

"Rest in peace, buddy. I know you're looking down at all of us right now and thinking, 'what a waste of time'. But we showed up anyway—because you mattered to us."

39: Influencers

Two college freshmen sat on a vinyl couch in the dorm lounge watching an old war movie late on a Saturday night.

"You know, Hitler wasn't all wrong.

"What?!"

"Yes, it is widely accepted."

"Accepted by whom? The man is universally considered to have been a monster."

"Accepted by leading authorities."

"Leading authorities, where?"

"On the internet—YouTubers, bloggers, university professor types. They have tons of likes and followers."

"You're an idiot."

"Well, I'm just saying it's out there. I didn't make it up."

"Well, somebody else did. He was a monster."

40: Cracked

Humpty Dumpty was not having a good day. He had been out until the wee hours of the morning with John Jacob Jingleheimer Schmidt, and that dude knows how to party. Does everyone in town know him? Apparently.

He was dead to the world when the phone rang at 6:00 a.m.

"Hello," he whispered as his yolk pounded in his shell.

"Hump, it's Bo Peep. I need your help. I've lost my sheep and don't know where to find them."

"Bo, baby, we've been over this before. Just leave them alone, they'll come home."

Then, the Big Bad Wolf blew in with some fresh bacon and invited Humpty over for breakfast. On the way, Humpty nearly tripped over three blind mice frantically zig-zagging down the sidewalk. There were no injuries, but it was too close for comfort.

Heading home from Wolfie's house, he spotted a spider stuck at the top of a water spout. Jack and Jill happened to walk by, and Humpty asked them to fetch a pail of water to wash the spider out.

Scatterbrained as always, Jack and Jill did not return. However, along came the rain and did the job. Unfortunately, the spider immediately ran inside and sat down beside Miss Muffet, who was eating her lunch. She screamed, blamed Humpty, and stormed off.

Still reeling from Muffet's meltdown, Humpty stepped into the street—just in time to nearly get scrambled by a pony. Yankee Doodle claimed he was distracted as he put a feather in his hat. That dandy was new in town and was not making a good first impression.

Still, there was excitement. Word spread that the King and his horses would soon be passing by on their way to the castle. A crowd gathered and pushed Humpty to the back. He couldn't see a thing.

"Let's climb the wall," suggested his friend Little Boy Blue, who had just awakened from his nap. In hindsight, this was probably not the best idea.

As the royal parade approached, Boy Blue let out a celebratory blast with his horn. Startled, Humpty lost his balance and had a great fall.

The King, all his horses, and all his men rushed to Humpty's aid. Sadly, all appeared lost. Humpty suffered multiple fractures and extensive internal injuries.

But what do all the King's horses and all the King's men know about such things? Did anyone even think about calling 911?

41: Sarcasm

The principal introduced the next speaker, "Students, please welcome Dean Lamont Snarq from the University of Iowa College of Sarcasm."

"Thank you, Ms. Duhlgreen. Students, I appreciate the opportunity to acquaint you with the University of Iowa College of Sarcasm. Our fully accredited college is an integrated component of the University system, offering Bachelor and Master of Fine Arts degrees in sarcasm. Our program is based on the traditional lessons and techniques of the European masters of sarcasm, which are far superior to the monotone condescension imparted by the elite American universities.

"The stand-alone degree is excellent preparation for careers in print and broadcast journalism, sports commentary, public service, and business. It is also the ideal undergraduate program for those planning to pursue professional degrees in law, medicine, and social work. Recognizing sarcasm as an essential element of all human interaction, we offer electives for undergraduates in the Colleges of Nursing, Engineering, Pharmacy, Liberal Arts, Education, and Public Health.

"At Iowa, our students receive comprehensive instruction in all major sarcastic disciplines: haughty, humorous, subtle, biting, ethnic, malignant, scholarly, sports, juvenile, faux, defensive, and pious sarcasm. The elements of sarcastic body language, including facial expressions, gestures, and posture, are explored and refined in small-group lab settings.

"Our curriculum is grounded in the belief that sarcasm is an art form, one that can only be mastered through rigorous instruction and diligent practice. We will beat you down and then build you back stronger and better. Sarcasm is the great equalizer, and in the hands of a skilled practitioner, it becomes a nuanced, delicate tool. In a world distinctly viewed through its lens, nothing looks the same.

"A broad selection of extracurricular activities provides an excellent opportunity to utilize and develop your evolving sarcastic skill set. This past year, our students notably impacted Student government, club sports, and Greek life.

"Our faculty is engaged in a wide range of scholarly research. Significant work in cooperation with the College of Education has resulted in the integration of sarcasm into the core curriculum for the degree in elementary education. Thus, equipping future educators with a unique foundation for shaping young minds—and neutralizing their parents.

"Our graduates are prepared to be leaders in the new world order, dedicated to coercion through the spoken and written word. The future of sarcasm is unlimited. I invite you to grasp that future by the *cojones*, or risk being the one whose *cojones* are grasped...

"...I beg your pardon; I realize the word *'cojones'* may be offensive to some. Please feel free to substitute 'toes' in its place...which, incidently, is an excellent example of passive-aggressive pious sarcasm. A topic I cover in detail in my YouTube TED talk, *Intro to the Sarcastic Non-Apology*."

42: A Cut

The coach opened the box and began to hand out the jerseys. On the back was their last name and a number. On the front was their team's name, Cougars, and beneath it a bold phrase, "No Regrets".

The coach explained that "No Regrets" would be the team motto this year. They were to leave it all on the field. Win or lose, there would be no complaints, no excuses, and above all…no regrets.

Alice felt a sick twist in her stomach. She *did* have regrets, a big one. It had nothing to do with soccer. Her regret was deeply personal. That phrase, stamped across her jersey, shouted back at her every time she looked down.

She had a younger sister, Stacy. They'd always been close, but Stacy was going through a stage where she was quite bluntly a "smart ass." Still, they were sisters. They loved and looked out for each other.

One day, Alice saw Stacy do something foolish and very dangerous. Her first instinct was to warn Stacy, to make her stop. But she didn't. She knew that any warning or criticism would result in a sarcastic response, something quite hurtful. Alice didn't want that, didn't need that. So, she said nothing.

A short while later, Stacy repeated the same stupid, dangerous act and tragically drowned. Alice was devastated. She kept replaying the moment that might have changed everything. If only she had said something.

This was compounded by her mother and father lamenting that if they had only known what Stacy was doing, they would have somehow prevented it. Alice could not share with her grieving parents what she had witnessed. She bore her guilt and grief alone.

Before each game, the team would put their hands in the center of a huddle and break with the chant, "No Regrets!" Each time they chanted it, the words slammed into her, her chest tightened, and her thoughts spiraled. Alice would instinctively cringe.

The Coach noticed. She had known Alice for years and sensed her pain. In a private moment, she pulled Alice aside. Alice suddenly felt she could open up. The coach listened intently, and tears gathered in the corners of her eyes.

"Alice, you need to talk to your mom and dad. You have a cut that is not going to heal on its own."

A broken family sat down together. One by one, they shared their grief, guilt, and pain. Together, they came to understand that the hardest person to forgive is yourself.

43: Our Words

There were times when Zack felt like he should say something significant—those important moments that felt destined to stay with him. Instead, he usually blurted out something trite or downright stupid. It made him wonder how all those famous people he'd read about in school always seemed to say just the right thing.

Lines like "I only regret that I have but one life to give for my country," or "Give me liberty or give me death," have lived on for more than two centuries. Zack couldn't believe those were spontaneous. Surely, Nathan Hale had a moment to think about his final words, testing different phrases in his mind before settling on that legendary line. Likewise, Patrick Henry probably spent some time at a Richmond tavern, kicking around ideas with his friends before delivering his immortal plea. People just didn't come up with profound declarations on the spur of the moment—at least not ordinary people like him.

Zack couldn't help but think back to his toast at his brother's wedding. "To my brother, my new sister-in-law, and all the hot bridesmaids," was probably inappropriate. Unfortunately, it's now part of family lore, though hardly the stuff of history books.

Perhaps those famous quotes were refined by historians and

admirers over the years. It wouldn't be the first-time people tried to paint a prettier face on their heroes. It seemed unlikely that any profound statement from a public figure was truly spontaneous.

Zack thought about it for a while, letting himself off the hook. Realizing that perfection rarely comes in the moment, and should the need arise, he would think things through ahead of time and practice.

"Our words may be spontaneous or profound," he thought, "but rarely are they both."

44: The Guard

Guillermo stood at the door. Never in his life had he expected to get this close to El Presidente. Still, there he was. El Presidente was shackled to the floor and the arms of a plain wooden chair. Small beads of sweat dripped from his forehead and there was a trickle of blood at the corner of his mouth.

The room measured no more than two and a half meters on each side. No windows, blank walls, and a single bare light bulb hanging from the ceiling. Two additional guards stood on either side of the prisoner.

He had always liked El Presidente. His village had a clean water spigot and several pole lights. A spider's nest of cords ran from each pole to the nearby huts. His father told him that all this was a gift from El Presidente, but others claimed that it was the work of the United Nations. He didn't care where it came from. He felt fortunate to grow up in such a modern place.

In school, Guillermo had learned that the hero, El Presidente, had saved the nation from the former corrupt leaders who had exploited the people for their own gain. Almost every home proudly displayed his picture.

He was surprised when he joined the Army that not everyone believed this. Some officers secretly worked to turn the people against El Presidente. They influenced newspapers and radio stations to report that El Presidente was stealing money from the people and abusing his power.

There was an uprising. The people and the military joined forces to storm the capital. El Presidente was captured. There would be a trial to expose his treachery.

From his post guarding the door, Guillermo watched Colonel Alvarez approach along the corridor.

"Private, you are relieved. You may return to the barracks."

Guillermo saluted, then stood aside as the Colonel entered the room.

As Guillermo walked down the hallway, a shot rang out behind him. He winced with surprise, then kept going.

The next morning, Guillermo learned that El Presidente had been shot while trying to escape. Colonel Alvarez was now El Presidente. He pledged to quickly clean up all the corruption and exploitation of the old regime.

Years later, Guillermo would tell his grandchildren the story of his cherished encounter with **two** El Presidentes. One had been seated only a couple of meters from him, and the other had actually spoken to him as he passed by.

Who would think that such a thing could happen to a boy from such a small village?

45: The Unpreventable

Lee was pale and shaky. He had been up and down all night, racked by waves of nausea, abdominal cramping, and relentless trips to the bathroom. Today was important, and he absolutely could not miss work. He struggled to get up, but his legs buckled beneath him. Dressing was not even an option.

He made the call. "I'm not going to make it. I'm too sick to even get out of bed," he whispered weakly into the phone. The voice on the other end was unsympathetic and insistent. Lee hung the phone up; he wasn't leaving his apartment. They would just have to do without him today.

In the bathroom, he found a glass bottle half filled with pink liquid and a spoon. Two tablespoons of the concoction coated his mouth and throat, thick and unpleasant to swallow. He promptly fell back into bed, too exhausted to fight off sleep.

Throughout the morning, Lee stirred and dragged himself out of bed for yet another trip to the bathroom. Around 10:30, he gave himself another dose of Pepto-Bismol, then collapsed back to sleep.

Around 1:00 p.m., his body aching, he could sleep no longer. He had to sit up. He dragged himself into the living room and slumped onto the vinyl couch. The Julie Benell Show came up on the black and white TV, an innocuous lifestyle commentary, a diversion. Then, abruptly, the program was interrupted.

[REPORT] Shots fired at the president's motorcade!

Lee stirred. Maybe it was the sound of the television, or perhaps the illness was finally passing. His eyes were bleary, but he was intently interested. He watched the scene unfold at Parkland Hospital and the announcement of the President's death.

There was no definite information on the assassin, although there were reports of a possible shooter on a "grassy knoll".

Lee watched the TV coverage late into the night. Alone and weakened by the flu, he was a spectator to a momentous episode in American history.

For the rest of his life, Lee Harvey Oswald would never forget that fateful day, November 22, 1963… and the sobering realization that history had unfolded without him.

46: Karma

It started with a chill shooting up my spine, then I was startled awake by a sound, and finally, the eerie feeling that I was being watched. It was probably nothing. Right?

Except I wasn't the only one. Others had an uneasiness, too.

A day or two went by before it all started to make sense. Sitting in the coffee shop, sipping a latte, I saw Jennifer "Fizzy" Razzle with Thorny Foster. They were all over each other, cuddling and kissing. It made me cringe. No way this was happening.

You have to understand, Fizzy is far and away the most desirable woman in town. Beautiful, intelligent, vivacious, and a successful executive at the bank. She could have, and probably has, had any man she wanted. It made no sense that she seemed to be attracted to Thorny.

It is charitable to say that Thorny is not much to look at. He is balding, with a scraggly beard, pot belly, bulging eyes, and a nose shaped like a question mark. He is barely smart enough to turn on a light and constantly drifts from one dead-end job to another.

Then, the realization hit me like a ton of bricks. This must be the Gates of Hell. Every kid around here grows up with the story of the

Gates of Hell. The go-to story for campouts or sleepovers is whispered in the dark as the uninitiated grow sleepy. Everyone swears they don't believe it, but nobody goes near the Boblett Cemetery after dark.

At the entrance to the cemetery stands a large arching iron gate, known locally as the Gates of Hell. Legend has it that if you stand beneath the arch at the stroke of midnight, the Devil will grant you one wish. Naturally, there is a catch, but not the "sell your soul" kind you would expect.

No, the Devil opens the graves. For twenty-four hours, the dead wander the earth. Some tend to unfinished business, some play tricks on the living, others just watch.

It's a terrifying thought for a seven or eight-year-old hearing the story for the first time. It is enough to make you flinch at shadows in the corners or jump when the wind rustles the leaves. More than one kid has spent the night shivering under the covers pulled tightly over their head. Childish fears, maybe, but part of our local rite of passage.

This… this was real. Now, I had proof that the story wasn't just a myth. How could Thorny have hooked up with Fizzy? Thorny must have visited the Gates of Hell.

It seems far-fetched…but then again, look at Thorny. Look at Fizzy. Can you think of a more logical explanation?

Thorny had unleashed the undead. Honestly, I really couldn't blame him. But then I remembered that Fizzy wasn't always perfect.

She was once…ordinary.

Could it be that Thorny wasn't the only one in that couple who had made a wish at the Gates of Hell? If it is, then the Devil has a wicked sense of humor.

Karma bites.

47: Juxtaposition

Louise and Ruby sat across from each other in the waiting room, awaiting their appointments.

Louise had arrived thirty minutes early, as usual. Her days were mostly empty now, and appointments gave her a sense of purpose. She was smartly dressed in an Armani suit with a single strand of Tiffany pearls. Her Louis Vuitton purse sat neatly on her lap, her arms tightly crossed over it. Her legs were forcefully crossed as well, exposing tasteful Gucci shoes. She eyed Ruby with quiet disdain.

Ruby tilted slightly to the left in her well-worn wheelchair with a cheerful expression on her face. She had lost her left leg just below the knee, and all the toes of her right foot were missing. Her baggy dress was soiled, and her hair was in disarray. She chatted with her grandson, genuinely interested in his report on a book he was reading.

The tech called Ruby back to the exam room.

"Ruby, how are you today?" the doctor asked.

"I am blessed," she replied with a sunny smile.

The doctor knew Ruby was raising her two adolescent grandchildren alone while her daughter served time in prison.

She had lost her leg and toes to the ravages of diabetes, and she was in kidney failure. Today, he had to tell her that the laser treatments and eye injections were no longer working. He would do everything he could, but she needed to prepare herself. She was going blind.

His heart broke when Ruby comforted him.

"Doctor, I just want to thank you for all you have done. God has always been good to me; I'll be just fine."

There were tears in his eyes as he entered the next room. There, Louise sat coiled like a cobra. Her mouth puckered in a sour expression. The doctor paused for a second, struck by the contrast with Ruby. Louise was a very wealthy widow in excellent health. To his knowledge, she lived a privileged life and lacked nothing.

"Good morning, Louise, how are you today?"

"About as well as can be expected," was her terse reply.

"I wish I could put you in a room alone with Ruby for five minutes," he instinctively thought.

Little did he know that he already had.

48: A Compatriot

He sat quietly in the afternoon's golden hour, trying to capture the unique colors of the landscape before the lighting faded. This was the third day that he had failed to match his palette to the scene before him. His frustration was obvious as he gathered up his supplies.

A well-dressed, muscular man with dark hair and a thick mustache observed him from nearby, "Done for the day?"

"Just debating whether to throw my paints in the river or myself," the artist replied, his voice raspy.

The stranger let out a soft chuckle, his eyes flickering with understanding. "I know that feeling. Let me buy you a drink, and we can talk it over."

Effortlessly, the stranger charmed the painter into revealing his story. He had an uneventful middle-class upbringing in Wisconsin. After three years at the university, he left to enlist in the Army. Gassing in the Meuse-Argonne resulted in serious lung damage. He returned home after the war, but could not see any future in the family lumber yard. He chose not to stay.

"At most, I have a few years to live, just days if I catch pneumonia. I asked myself whether I wanted the last thing I ever saw to be the lights of Paris or Racine. I said my goodbyes and came here."

"So, you chose the gloomy, cold, wet winters of Paris for your health then?" his new acquaintance said with a wry smile. "How is the starving artist's life going for you?"

"I paint. My work is critiqued. I try to improve, but to be honest, I don't have the talent to express what I envision. Strangely, I find pleasure in the effort, though. So, tell me about yourself."

The handsome stranger downed his drink and leaned in, "Raised in Chicago, I, too, was wounded in the war. Like you, I found it difficult to go home. Now I write a little and absorb the energy of this city. There's a group of fellow expatriates who often gather to celebrate our creativity and shared joy of just being alive. You should join us."

The artist grinned, "It is good to be alive, but for me, this is a deeply personal journey. For now, at least, I choose to go it alone. I am content to be anonymous today and forgotten tomorrow."

The writer extended his hand, "You are right, of course. A hundred years from now, no one will even know we were here. But if you change your mind, look me up. The name is Hemingway, Ernie Hemingway. Carpe diem, my friend."

49: A Guide

"Boss, would you mind if I clocked out 30 minutes early today? It's our anniversary, and I need a little extra time to clean up before going out to dinner."

"No problem, what year is this for you two?"

"It's our sixth. How long have you and Deloris been married?"

"It'll be forty-seven years this June."

"Wow, so tell me the secret to a long and happy marriage."

"Well, do you want a flippant answer or a serious one?"

"If you've got a serious one, I'll take it."

"Well, to be honest, I'm still figuring it out. But in my experience, when you're young, you fall in love with a body, you know, physical attraction. If that part is strong, you overlook a lot. But as you grow older, you fall in love with the person."

He continued, "Bodies change, that's no surprise. But so do people. Over time, you and your spouse start to think and act alike. Opposites may attract, but long-term couples smooth out those differences."

"Have you ever noticed how your parents seem to be very set in their ways?"

"Have I ever! They are so unrealistic."

"I'll bet they've changed their views plenty over the years. What you're seeing now is the result of years of shared experiences. They've worked things out together, made adjustments, and found what works for them as a team."

He paused and smiled kindly.

"Eventually, you come to love the person who has shared your experiences, supported you through good times and bad. It's a foundation that can be relied upon for whatever the future brings."

"Surely, that doesn't mean that you and Deloris see eye to eye on everything?"

"No way, we're only human," he said with a laugh. "We argue a lot and sometimes quite intensely. When you love the person, you know you'll get through it. You forgive. You move forward."

"Thanks, boss. Most people would just give the usual, 'Happy wife, happy life,' or 'Never go to bed angry.' You gave me something real, something worth thinking about."

"Anytime, now get out of here before you blow year six."

50: The Message

It should have been a stunning announcement, but instead it was met with a resounding, "I told you so." The voice was heard by everyone, everywhere at the same time. For each, it was a comforting, familiar voice in their own language.

The message was simple: *"Do not be afraid. We are among you. We have always been among you. We gave you a moral code and have passively observed your struggles to abide by it. You are in danger. Abide by the code."*

Some heard the voice of God. Others perceived an alien encounter. A few claimed mass hysteria and denied that it had happened at all. Regardless of interpretation, the world was no longer the same.

What once had been ideological differences escalated into violent extremism, with factions perceiving any opposition as being the ultimate threat to humanity. Us versus them, good versus evil, right versus wrong. Each side was attempting to force its will on the other. In that moment, the core of the message was buried beneath the need to be right.

Lost in the reaction was any examination of the moral code. What did it even mean to "abide by the code"? What had they failed to do that had placed them in danger?

The second message was anything but comforting: *"The danger you face is of your own making. Find commonality, or face destruction. Abide by the code."*

Some tried to promote cooperation and compromise. Their efforts were obstructed by others obsessed with their cause, who doubled down in their opposition.

The final message was simple and impactful: *"You could not manage to get along, therefore you shall all be dependent on each other."*

Suddenly, everyone, everywhere, lost their sight. Survival required trusting, respecting, and loving each other. Those who would not…were lost.

51: Self-Aware

"Did you hear that idiot on the news last night going on about the economy?"

"I don't know how some people can be so out of touch. What world are they living in?"

"Yeah, I honestly don't mind if people have opinions different from mine, as long as they aren't spreading lies."

"Exactly, we should allow those people to express themselves—as long as they're apologetic about it. I mean, they must know how offensive their views are."

"You're right, of course. Freedom of speech and all that, but there should be limits. We should all be able to agree that some ideas are not only wrong, they're dangerous."

"Reasonable boundaries are just common sense. They exist for the common good."

"Exactly, and if they cross those lines…"

"Then we cancel them!"

52: The Sea

The South Pacific night was hot, and the sea was rough. Temperatures that day had approached 100 degrees, and the ship retained the heat like an oven belowdecks. Topside offered the Marine and several sailors a cooler respite. He slept on a blanket with his head on his life jacket. The night was dark, and the ship's hull made a "whooshing" sound as it cut through the waves.

As these men slept, the galley crew below rattled dishes as they went about their duty. The sound carried for miles through the water, where it was picked up by the sonar operator of an enemy submarine. The sub-commander peered through his night periscope, sweeping 360 degrees. He identified no ships. He ordered the boat to surface.

The submarine breached the surface, and the captain climbed to the bridge. Due east, he detected a dark silhouette through his binoculars, heading straight for him. At a distance of ten miles, the object was too small to identify. He ordered the sub to submerge to periscope depth. The cat would sneak up on its prey.

A heavy cruiser with no destroyer escort was a sitting duck. It sailed a straight course, convinced the area was free of any enemy threat. The submarine approached and maneuvered to allow for a broadside shot. The torpedoes were fired at three to four-second intervals. They would intercept the cruiser in less than a minute.

The starboard bow suddenly became a mass of flying debris. Massive quantities of fuel flooded into the sea. The second torpedo hit the midship powder magazine. The ship and the sea erupted in flames.

The Marine and the sailors who slept around him were violently thrown into the air. Confused, they instinctively attempted to report to their stations. The ship began to list to starboard. No one heard an order to abandon ship. It became the obvious move. Within minutes, the ship slipped below the waves, taking 300 men with it.

The Marine floated in a group with several sailors. Similar clusters of survivors were spread by the waves over a large area. The thick oil on the water coated his body and burned his eyes and throat. He had no idea that no one would come looking for them. His ship had been on a secret mission. No distress signal had gone out.

It was a big ocean, and the family farm in Illinois was a million miles away. He would struggle to survive as long as possible, but he understood that there was little hope. He found comfort in the ship's Catholic chaplain, who courageously moved from group to group ministering as best he could.

"O hear us when we cry to Thee, For those in peril on the sea."

53: Dark Secret

It was totally safe. She knew that, but it didn't make any difference. There was nothing rational about her fear. She could not, by her own reason or strength, reverse the curse. She was afraid of the dark.

Sleepovers, hide and seek, and stargazing were all things she avoided. Her entire life, she had adapted her circumstances and environment to avoid the terror of being alone in the dark. Now her high school children had designed the school's Halloween haunted house. She tried to decline the "privilege" of free admission, but they were too proud of their hard work for her to refuse.

A five-hundred-foot maze filled with over fifty macabre scenes and multiple surprises, all in total darkness. This certainly had to violate multiple OSHA regulations. What about fire codes? Was it ADA compliant? She hated that these thoughts were even entering her mind. She was despicable, but still, she couldn't help it.

This was a fundraiser for her kids, who had worked so passionately on it. She needed to put motherhood above her phobia. She just had to "woman up" and do it.

The line was long, and there was a possibility of a power failure or maybe an injury that would close it down. To her disappointment, progress was uneventful. At the entrance, a "guide" dressed as a zombie ushered her into a small, dimly lit room. Then she passed through a curtain and was instantly swallowed by total darkness. She pulled a small penlight from her pocket and advanced cautiously. Around a sharp right-hand turn, a large green rubber hand grabbed her flashlight.

"No cheating!" said a deep, gruff voice.

In an instant, she had lost her last lifeline; then she was in total darkness again. She tried to advance, but her legs were frozen. A small, flickering shape darted past, its bristly fur tickling her ankle like a spectral threat. She shrieked and collapsed against a wall. Paralyzed, hyperventilating, and sobbing, she became just another of the "scenes" as other guests groped their way past her.

Mercifully, someone came along and offered to escort her to the "chicken" exit. She burst through the door into the gorgeous, dim light of the parking lot. She was alive. She had done it.

"Best haunted house ever!" she exclaimed to her kids; her voice obviously shaky.

"We knew you'd like it. Want to go again tomorrow night?"

54: The Prenup

Mack invited Al into his man cave and pointed to a comfy chair. "Just wanted to get to know you a little better. I want you to know that Lana's my favorite daughter, but please don't tell her sisters," he said with a wide grin. Then earnestly added, "Mind if I ask a few questions?"

"No, it's nice to get a chance to know you as well," Al replied nervously, squirming ever so slightly.

"What was Roger Maris' batting average in 1961, and how many times was he intentionally walked?"

"He batted .269 and had no intentional walks. I mean, why would you with Mantle batting right behind him?"

A slight grin turned the corners of Mack's mouth. "Where did Eddie Podolak go to high school, and what position did he play in college?"

"Podolak graduated from high school in Atlantic, Iowa. He played quarterback for two years and running back for one at the University of Iowa."

"Winningest coach for the Packers?"

"Curly Lambeau coached the Packers for nearly thirty years and had 209 victories."

"Who did Brett Favre play for after he left the Packers?"

"I don't know, why would anyone care what he did after he left the Packers?"

Mack's demeanor softened noticeably. "Okay, smart guy, who was the last guy to wear #33 for the Celtics before Larry Bird?"

"I could be wrong, but I think it was Steve Kuberski. He retired a couple of seasons before Bird arrived, and I don't think anyone else had that number in between.

Mack gave Al a sly smile. "Last question," he said.

The muscles in Al's back tensed, and his mouth went dry.

"How many World Series have the Yankees been in?"

"All of them, it is not an official World Series if the Yankees are not in it!"

Mack's brow tightly furrowed... Then he broke into a hearty laugh. "Welcome to the family, Al. I think you'll do just fine."

"Thank God for the cheat sheet Lana gave me," Al thought to himself.

55: The Maxim

Growing up, the brothers had heard it so often that they cringed when they sensed it was coming.

"If life were easy, everyone would do it."

It was their dad's catch-all phrase. He used it indiscriminately for any major or minor complaint. Anything from breaking an arm to missing the school bus warranted the "If life were easy…"

It had become trite. What the heck did he mean by it anyway? None of them had ever asked. There was always a vague sense that it meant "toughen up" or "get over it," but no one ever got a clear explanation.

Now with young families of their own, the brothers gathered to celebrate the birthday of Tony's son.

Little Leland fell down and bumped his head on a coffee table. Naturally, he cried and ran to his mother. She kissed the sore spot and sent him back to play.

"It's not fair. I was having fun. That danged table; I hate it!" Leland exclaimed.

Then, without even thinking about what he was doing, Tony said, "Leland, if life were easy, everyone would do it."

"Where did that come from?" his wife, Karla, shot back. "What does that even mean?"

"Oh, our dad used to say that all the time," Tony's brother Hank offered.

"So," Karla continued, "whatever deep philosophical meaning it has is probably wasted on a four-year-old. Truthfully, I doubt if any of you guys even know what it means."

"Well, I always took it to mean that life is not easy for anyone and never has been," interjected the oldest brother, Steve.

"And never will be," noted Hank.

"Also, you don't know my problems and I don't know yours, but we all have them," Tony said, seeming to suddenly understand for the first time.

"Again, how was this appropriate for a four-year-old?" Karla persisted.

"Well, it probably wasn't. It just slipped out. However, is four too young to have it pointed out that a little bump on the head is not the worst thing in the world?"

"Yes, it is. Let him be a little boy—at least until he starts school!" Karla said, her tone annoyed and her look signaling the end of the discussion.

"Life won't be any easier then," Tony thought—but wisely didn't say

out loud. They'd revisit the maxim a little further down the road. There would come a time when even Karla would say it—maybe not out loud, but certainly think it.

56: Normal

"Aretha, how long have you been divorced, honey?"

"I'm not divorced. My husband has been a POW for nearly five years. Where did you get the idea, I was divorced?"

"I'm sorry, I must have misunderstood. I thought Sasha had told Melina that you were divorced."

Later that evening, "Sasha, would you come in here, please? Mrs. Lewis asked me today how long I've been divorced. Did you tell Melina that I was divorced?"

"Yes, Mama."

"Why on earth would you do such a thing, child?"

"I just want to be normal. No one else's daddy is a prisoner. I didn't want to be different."

"Honey, your daddy is a prisoner of war. He's a hero. You're not different, you're special."

"I don't want to be special. I just want to blend in. Lots of kids don't have dads because their moms are divorced."

Aretha softly sighed and gently twisted a dish towel in her hands. "Sasha, that is not fair to your daddy, and it's not fair to me. A lie is never the right answer. You need to tell your friends the truth."

"Mama, you don't understand… if you are divorced, I'm just like half my class. Having a dad who's a POW makes me like no one else."

"You're not ashamed of your daddy, are you?" she asked, slightly puzzled.

"I'm not ashamed, just mostly shy. I don't fit in, and this just makes it worse."

"Would it help if I spoke to your teacher or maybe the school counselor?"

"No, please don't! Can't we just leave this alone?"

"Would it be OK if I talked to someone at the Air Force base? They probably have encountered this before and could give me some advice."

"I suppose, but I doubt that they can do anything to help. Just please don't talk to anyone at school."

"Okay, come here and let me give you a hug. Why don't we write your daddy a letter and let him know we're thinking about him?"

A tear flowed down Aretha's cheek—the tear of a mother and the tear of a wife.

57: Whoops

The telephone rings.

"Hello."

"You got the money?"

"Sorry, I think you have the wrong number."

"Don't mess with me, man! Either you got the money or she dies."

"Seriously, you have the wrong number."

"You want her to die? 'Cause I'll kill her right now. Do…you…have…the…money?"

"I don't know who you are. I don't have any idea what you're talking about. I'm going to hang up."

An urgent female voice pleads: "Jack, don't hang up! He's serious. He'll kill me if you don't get him the money."

"I'm not Jack. Whoever you are, you dialed the wrong number. I'm going to hang up, and you should try dialing the number again."

Click… Ring.

"Jack, you better have the money!"

Now exasperated voice: "Listen, you are absolutely the worst kidnapper in the world. You can't even get the telephone number right for your ransom demands. Did you even write the number down?"

"Well, no."

"OK, did you ever think about asking your kidnap victim for Jack's number?"

"Uh, no."

"Listen, crap for brains, do that. Call him—and don't you dare call me again! Do you hear me? Not one more call to this number!"

"Sorry to bother you. Uh… have a nice day."

Click.

58: Gotcha

Tyrone was beyond angry; he was obsessed. Tonight, he was going to put an end to the whole issue. He was going to catch him in the act.

Like most of the working world, Tyrone was in bed by 10:00 and up by 6:00 every day. Being jolted awake at 2:00 a.m. by the rattling of trash cans had quickly gotten old.

Seriously, who was up at 2:00 in the morning anyway?

At first, he politely asked his neighbor to take the trash out earlier in the evening. Then, he became more forceful and threatened to bring the issue up before the homeowners' association. Each time, the neighbor refused to accept responsibility and insisted that he was not at fault.

He considered himself a patient man, but a month was long enough.

Tyrone dressed in his work clothes and lay on top of the bedcovers. His large industrial-grade flashlight was within reach on his bedside table.

As per schedule, there was a sharp clatter of metal lids banging against the pavement. The clock read 2:07.

Tyrone was instantly on his feet, flashlight in hand. With a few strides, he was out the door and heading for the driveway. He could see movement at the trash cans.

"Gotcha!" he yelled as he swung his flashlight on the culprit.

Several raccoons scattered in the bright light. One very large raccoon took particular offense at being disturbed. He stood up on his hind legs, baring sharp teeth, his eyes glowing in the light.

Tyrone suddenly felt very small … in more ways than one. The flashlight slipped from his grasp and rolled down the driveway.

"You win, little buddy," he whispered as he made a hasty retreat to the comfort and safety of his bed.

59: Suddenly

I never thought much about it. I always assumed I would be safe in my own home, my own bed. Wouldn't you?

It was so sudden that I had no response, except for perhaps a slight gasp as I awoke just before the blow. Then it was over. I have no recognition of my attacker. There was a shadow and movement followed by a sudden clarity that I was dead.

I am aware that Sam suffered a similar fate, but I feel no anger or grief. I honestly cannot identify any emotion, except perhaps curiosity—if that is an emotion. I am confused—what happened, why, and who did it?

Sam says he felt certain he could protect me. That's what husbands are supposed to do. But obviously, he couldn't. Again, he states it as a matter of fact with no regret or rage.

Our perspective is as observers of the world we left behind. We are able to witness but not interact—detached from events and even our mortal remains. Strangest of all is our indifference to the living: family, friends, and enemies alike.

We are—or were—a Christian family. Shouldn't we be in Heaven? I don't really understand why we're here, but I am not worried—again, just not what I expected. I still trust in God's promise. Whatever this is, it's certainly not Hell. It's also not "nothingness", or whatever atheists expect. For some reason, we will be spectators as the living deal with the grief of our murder and try to figure out who did it. I am suddenly struck with the wish that I could communicate to the living that they have nothing to fear from ghosts. If we *are* indeed ghosts, we have no ability to reach back into our former existence.

In the home we left behind, the only survivor is our family dog, Max. Locked in the pantry near the kitchen, he barks and scratches at the door. He's made a mess of the canned goods and supplies I had meticulously organized on the lower shelves. Now he desperately wants out. He cannot understand why he has been trapped in there.

Next door, Ida and Dwight Cooper have just finished breakfast. Dwight is perturbed by the racket Max is making. He trudges over to our house and climbs the three steps to the front porch. Two firm knocks on the front door go unanswered. Dwight decides to try the back door by the kitchen. He stops just short of the kitchen door. It is ajar. Something is not right. He slowly nudges the door open and gasps, "Aaah!"

Ida sees him running back and meets him at the door. "There is blood everywhere!" he sobs, collapsing into her arms.

60: Faith

She had slept in and was still in bed when a soft knock sounded on her bedroom door.

"You okay in there?" her father asked.

"Yeah, I'm fine. Just getting up."

She stretched, sighed, and reluctantly pulled herself out of bed. As she dressed, she could already hear her parents moving around downstairs, the familiar clatter of dishes and quiet hum of conversation.

By the time she entered the kitchen, her mother was slicing tomatoes for sandwiches. The smell of fresh coffee lingered in the air.

Her father glanced up from his seat at the table. "Got a minute to talk?"

She hesitated. "About what?"

He set his coffee mug down. "Just wondered why you didn't want to go to church with us this morning."

She exhaled sharply, bracing for the scolding. "You wouldn't understand."

Her father leaned back in his chair. "Try me."

She shifted her weight, crossing her arms. "It's just … none of my professors, and hardly any of my classmates, believe in God. I've been studying evolution, and I have to admit that I'm having doubts about creation, about God."

Her father nodded slowly, unsurprised. "I understand."

She frowned, "Do you?"

"It's reasonable to question things when almost everyone around you does," he said. "I imagine it feels like you're standing alone."

She stared at the floor, surprised that he wasn't immediately trying to shut her down. "Yeah, it does."

Her father took a sip of coffee, "A lot of your professors and classmates see faith as irrational because they've already dismissed the possibility of God. They're only looking at one side of the argument. And your textbooks present evolution as fact, but it's still a theory. One that leaves plenty of unanswered questions."

She shifted uncomfortably, "I don't know. Science makes sense. I can't just argue the Bible against everything I'm learning."

"You don't have to," he said. "Faith and science don't have to be enemies. You'll have to learn what's required to pass your classes. College is like that. But that doesn't mean you have to abandon your faith. You can question, you can wrestle with things, and you can seek answers." He paused, his voice gentle, "God isn't afraid of your doubts."

She swallowed hard. She hadn't expected this conversation to feel … comforting. Usually, she tuned out her dad's lectures, but this time, something in his words penetrated.

"I just… don't know anymore," she said again, softer this time.

"You don't have to figure it all out today," he said, standing and pressing a kiss to the top of her head as he passed. "Just don't stop searching."

She watched him go, thoughtful. Maybe talking to him wasn't a total waste of time after all.

61: The Answer

The great minds of the century had been gathered together to consider 20 questions. The moderator began, "Are right and wrong just two sides of the same coin?"

"Why a coin and not a brick?" Camille pondered.

"Exactly; this is not a binary choice." Jean Pierre interjected, "A brick is six-sided, representing the multifaceted nature of the true question."

Alfred offered, "We should not limit the consideration to the rigid form of a brick; certainly, the malleability of a sponge would better represent the fluidity that is the essence of the issue."

"Do not ignore the obvious. Bricks are unstable without mortar," Sir Thomas declared.

Somewhat annoyed, the moderator asked, "Could we please move past bricks and consider the question at hand regarding right and wrong?"

"Of course," Alfred responded, "Movement is the dilemma in distinguishing right from wrong. Once again, fluidity is the essence of the issue."

Dr. Chin thoughtfully observed, "There is a continuum with right at one extreme and wrong at the other, much like a string."

"Yes, yes, excellent," Sir Thomas exploded. "Question answered. There is no definitive right or wrong, just a position on a scale."

Camille objected, "Dr. Chin's 'String Theory' is ambiguous. I agree a string can be multifaceted, fluid, and bind together opposing positions; but a fixed position on a string does not allow for differences in perception of where that position is."

"You lost me there, Camille," a grinning Jean Pierre said.

"Well, I think you have offensive body odor, but Alfred does not. The position on the string is relative to perception," Camille responded with a devious chuckle.

Once again, the moderator interjected, "We have moved from bricks to string, but have we answered the question?"

Sir Thomas exclaimed, "I need a short break. This has been entirely too strenuous!"

Abdula, who had been silently observing, finally spoke. "Is there even any point in continuing the discussion?"

The moderator replied weakly, "No."

A young child in the audience asked in a loud voice, "Isn't the answer they're looking for just *yes*?"

62: Left Behind

The father walked slowly, sometimes carrying his tiny daughter, sometimes letting her walk beside him, holding his hand. Fifteen years had passed since the end of the war, but the dirt road was still deeply rutted and the countryside scarred. He dreaded what he was about to do and several times nearly turned back. It was for her own good. Someday, she would thank him. He kept telling himself it had to be done.

They arrived at the orphanage and were met by a stern-looking woman. The father explained that he had a large family and could not provide for everyone. She was the smallest and most vulnerable of his children. He pleaded with the staff to take her in and find her a better home. He completed the paperwork and hugged her for the last time.

She hadn't seen the tears in his eyes as he left her behind. She would never see her father again. He would eventually secure a good job and be able to provide a comfortable life for his family. Her family would always wonder what happened to their sweet little girl. Did she remember them? Did she feel rejected or abandoned? Thoughts of how scared, lonely, sad she must have been tormented them.

The orphanage did provide regular meals, clean clothes, and a safe place to sleep. Although the adults were not cruel, neither were they kind or loving. There were no emotional attachments, no hugs, and no bedtime stories. What could have been joyful years of youthful innocence were lost to a monotonous life of benign indifference.

Because she was quite small, the orphanage changed her records. She was assigned a new birthday, cutting two years off her age. A younger child was more likely to be placed. The deception may have helped, as she was one of the fortunate children to be adopted.

The "seven"-year-old traveled halfway around the world to join a new mother, father, and set of brothers and sisters. She neither spoke their language nor looked like them, but she had a loving family. She also had limitless opportunity—the support to go as far as her intelligence, ability, and ambition allowed.

Thousands of miles away, a father never knew the outcome of his sacrifice and was forever troubled by whether he had done the right thing for his sweet little girl.

63: The Liar

The assistant in the county clerk's office collected the forms and stapled them together. She handed them to a distinguished man in his sixties, who thanked her and turned for the door. He gathered two well-behaved young children from the chairs against the wall as he departed.

"Grandpa, where did the stapler come from?" the four-year-old asked as they walked down the sidewalk.

"Well, a long time ago, there was a little boy named Hank Sharples, and his mother had all kinds of papers that she needed to keep organized. She tried paper clips, but they kept slipping off.

"She tried pinning them together with a straight pin, but she kept pricking her finger and getting blood all over her papers. Hank suggested bending the pins under, but this took a lot of time.

"Hank was very clever, and he experimented with ways to poke the pin through the paper and bend the ends. It took him many attempts. He started with a pin that was U-shaped and sharp on both ends. Then he had to develop a way to hold and insert the pins. The machine he invented to do this was the stapler."

"But Grandpa, why is it called a stapler?"

"Well, at first it was called the 'sharpler', after little Hank Sharples. But people confused the 'sharpler' with the pencil sharpener. So, it was decided that it would be called the stapler."

"Excuse me," interrupted a strange woman walking behind them. "I find it highly offensive to blatantly lie to these young children. You should be ashamed of yourself."

Grandpa turned and looked at the stranger. "I apologize for offending you. I didn't realize that you were eavesdropping on our conversation. Had I known, I would have certainly begun my explanation with the fasteners designed for Louis XV of France; included the advancements patented by Slocum, Jillion, and McGill; and finished with the ultimate contribution of Henry Heyl. I just thought that a documentary might be a little dry and advanced for a three and four-year-old. Instead, I opted for a fairy tale."

The stranger frowned. "I don't appreciate your sarcasm! I am a strong advocate for children. Lying to these children like that is a form of psychological abuse. I would be within my rights to report you to the authorities!"

"Please, make that call," Grandpa said with a gentle smile as he offered her his phone.

The woman pushed the phone away with an angry scowl and briskly walked away.

"She was rude," said the three-year-old. "I like your stories."

"She should mind her own business," said the four-year-old. "We're not stupid. Grandma told us that all your stories are full of crap."

64: The Sham

Contrary to the public perception, the network's evening celebrity interview segments are often anything but glamorous. Ashanti absolutely did not want to do this interview. She viewed Marsha Manning as the embodiment of everything wrong with Hollywood. But the decision was not hers. As a professional, she would do what her job required.

Ms. Manning kept everyone waiting for nearly an hour. She refused to leave her dressing room until her makeup and clothing were perfect. In her twenties, Marsha Manning was considered one of the most beautiful women in the world. Now in her mid-forties, she was what is known in the trade as a ten-footer. From ten feet away, she was stunning, but up close, she looked unmistakably age-appropriate. A wide shot and soft lighting could still hide that. The crew passive-aggressively adjusted the lighting and focus to highlight her imperfections.

Once they were seated facing each other, Ashanti asked her first question. "Marsha, tell me why this role appealed to you."

"Ashanti, during my journey on the astral plane, I became aware of the subtle corners of a sphere. This enables me to perceive the locus of each project or role on the time-space continuum." Marsha answered in a soft, whispery voice—part Marilyn Monroe, part Jackie Kennedy.

That inflection might have been deemed sensual decades ago, but now it struck Ashanti and the crew as affected and annoying.

"You lost me there. Are you saying spheres have corners?"

"All smooth exteriors, when examined under extreme scrutiny, will reveal a rough, jagged surface. When we similarly examine everything around us, we see that we are surrounded by a giant jigsaw puzzle. Each piece has only one place where it fits."

"Were you taking drugs when you 'discovered' this?"

"In my youth, I employed medicinal enhancement to relax my inhibitions and to be fully receptive to all that is revealed by the celestial spheres."

"Marsha, from where I'm sitting, it appears the medicinal enhancement has not quite worn off yet."

In the control booth, the producer nearly cut the interview off. Instead, he paused to see where this would go next.

Marsha's voice suddenly took on a coarse, malicious tone, "Careful, Honey, you are dangerously close to me walking." She looked up at the control booth and said, "Edit that last little bit out, please."

"Thank you very much, Ms. Manning. We have all that we need," the producer responded.

With a look of puzzlement, Marsha turned back to Ashanti, who had already dropped her mic on the chair and walked away.

65: The Beautician

Shirley, a high school sophomore, arrived for her 2:30 appointment and settled into the chair. The beautician draped the cape around Shirley's neck and asked if she wanted the same haircut or something different.

"Well," Shirley hesitated, "there is a boy that I'd like to ask me to the Homecoming Dance. Do you think a new style will help?"

She laughed. "You might be surprised. Let's try a little more flair. I think that might just tip things in your favor."

The beautician turned the chair toward the mirror. Shirley caught her first look at her transformation and gasped—she was actually cute. If this didn't get Matt to notice her, nothing would.

Matt saw Shirley down the hall by her locker. He walked up, smiled, and commented on her new look. He liked it. They chatted, and he asked her if she had a date for Homecoming yet. And just like that, she did.

Elaine also complimented Shirley's new hairstyle. She asked who Shirley had gone to, since she was unhappy with her current stylist.

"You mentioned that you weren't pleased with your current style," the beautician said to Elaine.

"It's too youthful. I've been interviewing for part-time jobs, and appearing more mature would be helpful."

"That's very perceptive of you, Elaine. Let me see if I can help with that," the beautician said with empathy.

A few days later, Shirley was surprised to see Elaine working the cash register at the convenience store. Elaine was certain that her new look had helped her get the job.

Homecoming was almost too perfect: the dress, the new look, and Matt. Unfortunately, the date wasn't the thrill that Shirley had imagined. Matt turned out to be a total jerk, ditching her for most of the dance to hang with his football buddies.

During her next visit to the beautician, Shirley was asked whether her new style had worked out as she'd wanted.

Impulsively, she replied, "My hair is fine. It's that my date, Matt, turned out to be a real creep. I wish he were dead."

That night, Matt wrecked his motorcycle in a crash that nearly killed him.

Suddenly, Shirley realized that she and Elaine had both confided their secret desires to the beautician, and somehow things happened. In a panic, she phoned the beautician and begged her not to harm Matt again.

The beautician only laughed. "Silly girl, it's just a coincidence.

Haven't you noticed; they happen all the time."

66: Bunny

Corinne and her friends had been playing in the yard when they noticed it. A baby bunny was lying scared and injured in the tall grass. One of them must have accidentally stepped on it. Its little leg looked crooked, and the poor thing couldn't hop.

They took it into the house and asked Corinne's mom how to help. She found a shoebox and padded it with an old washcloth. It certainly looked like the right leg was broken. They reasoned that it should be supported and fashioned a splint from some popsicle sticks and tape.

They placed some shredded lettuce and water in the box. The tiny bunny did not attempt to eat the lettuce. They thought that it might be too young for lettuce. The friends took turns feeding it milk with an eye dropper.

The bunny needed a name, and there was quite a bit of discussion before the neighborhood children agreed on Wendy. They made a schedule, taking turns caring for Wendy at their homes. All their parents agreed that the responsibility of feeding and cleaning up after Wendy was a good lesson for the girls.

Sally's dad was the first one to mention that they could only keep Wendy long enough for her to heal. It was not fair to Wendy to keep her confined in a house. She needed to be outside and free to run—or hop.

This was a difficult thing for the girls to accept. Each of them had become very attached to Wendy and thought of her as a pet. With time, each of the parents worked with their daughters to help them understand that this was best for Wendy.

The splint had been on for six weeks when they removed it. Wendy was hesitant to use her leg. Elaine's mother explained that Wendy would need "physical therapy" to learn how to use her leg again. The girls enthusiastically undertook Wendy's rehabilitation.

Three weeks of conscientious "therapy" resulted in Wendy being able to hop around with no noticeable difficulty. The moment that they had been dreading had arrived.

Again, each of the parents stressed how it was the kindest thing to allow Wendy to live a proper bunny life. It was agreed that they would take Wendy to the park on Sunday and release her.

Sunday morning arrived, and all the girls and their parents participated in the event. The girls each said their tearful goodbyes and then released Wendy. As the girls proudly watched the result of their love and hard work, Wendy eagerly hopped toward the tall grass near the trees.

There was a sudden burst of movement as a hawk swooped down and snatched Wendy from the grass. Then she was gone.

67: Legacy

He was the son of a genuine rock and roll legend—four platinum albums, six Grammys, and two all-time classic rock anthems, capped off by the obligatory drug-related death at age 27, sealing his place in the infamous "27 Club." He bore his father's name, but he barely remembered him. Just five years old when his father died, he grew up with his mother far from the rock and roll life.

His mom and dad had known each other since second grade. They married after high school. She became a nurse, anticipating the need for a steady income while he pursued his music career. Through the years, she was the quiet anchor holding their small family together. Neither expected his spectacular rise to superstardom nor his tragic end in a San Francisco hotel room.

A young widow with a kindergartener, she fell back on Plan B: nursing. Although the royalties alone could have comfortably supported them, the work comforted her and provided a stable foundation for her young son.

Although it seemed that he was seldom out of earshot of his father's songs, the son never exhibited either talent or interest in music. He did, however, possess a fascination with mathematics. His mother was quietly relieved that he was choosing a different path and tenderly encouraged his interest. She cherished her husband's legacy, but shielded her son from the darker side.

He earned his undergraduate degree at Yale and a PhD in applied mathematics from MIT. His doctoral thesis prompted prestigious offers in both academia and the private sector. In the world of mathematics, he was a rising star.

Instead, he chose to disappear. Not literally, he simply chose a life of modesty and anonymity. He became an assistant professor at a small private college. He was exceptionally aware of how celebrity and hubris had destroyed his father's life. He would not allow himself to fall victim to those temptations.

Surprisingly, no one gave a second thought to his name. It was regarded as just a coincidence. The possibility that the nerdy professor was even remotely related to a Rock and Roll Hall of Famer was inconceivable. He had truly moved out from his father's shadow.

In time, he fell in love with an equally non-pretentious woman. He struggled with how to tell her he was the son of a rock icon and heir to his fortune. He agonized that his secret would somehow change how she saw him—or even worse, that she might be tempted by the allure of money and notoriety.

Their love grew stronger, and he knew that he had to tell her. She deserved to know the truth.

It happened over coffee on a relaxed Sunday morning. He looked tentatively into her eyes and acknowledged his father, silently apprehensive of her response.

"Oh," she said, "please don't take this the wrong way, but I don't know who that was."

68: Awakening

The King opened his eyes to his brightly sunlit bedchamber. He sensed that something was odd, but it did not quite register. The castle was too still, eerily so.

He sat up in bed. The fire in the hearth had burned out, and a chill filled the room. No footsteps shuffled on the stone hallway floors. No scent of bread drifted up from the kitchen. No bustle arose from the village below his window—only the sound of a gentle breeze rippling through the tapestries.

"Barclay, bring my robe!" he called out into the void.

Necessity overcame annoyance. Action was required. His feet hit the cold stone, and he located his robe draped across the foot of his bed. He tiptoed to a chamber pot behind a brocade screen in the corner. This was most distressing. Barclay's comfortable life, he mused grimly, was about to change.

He located his slippers, tightly secured his robe, and ventured into the hall. His heart suddenly sank. The Royal Guards were absent as well. Was he in danger? There was no evidence of a struggle or violence.

Cautiously, he crept into the Great Hall. Again, there were no guards, no courtiers, no valets, no pages. Where was everyone?

Equally fearful and curious, he continued to the kitchen. The table that should have been cluttered with the preparation of his morning meal was barren. The hearth was cold, and the cooks and kitchen maids were absent.

His booming voice echoed off the walls, "Hark! This is your King. Present yourselves at once!"

"I demand that you present yourselves—at once!" he repeated.

What has happened? he thought. Where has everyone gone? What will I do? I am the King. What will I do?

He stumbled to the castle courtyard. The drawbridge was down. He ventured into the village still dressed in his robe and slippers.

The villagers paid him no heed, just the polite distance afforded a madman.

"What has happened at the castle?" he demanded. "Where has everyone gone?"

The people looked upon the strange, bedraggled man, bewildered by his question. Construction on the *"King's Castle"* had been completed weeks ago. The amusement park would not open until next month.

69: Simple

Most everyone calls me Simple. Ordinary, I don't talk much. Most of what folks say takes a bit for me to understand. I'm just not quick, but I wanna tell you a story.

My friend Terry only had one arm. His left arm was just a little stump. He could do almost everything. He could eat, write, drive a car, and even fish with his other arm. We used to go fishing a lot. Terry was older than me, but he was my friend.

He belonged to the Disabled American Veterans. He had a DAV jacket, a DAV cap, and even a DAV license plate on his car. He was real proud of the DAV. He said they did a lot of good things.

One time, I asked Terry about his arm. You know, how he ended up with just a stump. He said it was an odd story.

Seems that he was in the Army. His job was shooting cannons and such. They were real loud and it hurt his ears. The Army said he lost some of his hearing. Because he didn't hear so good, he could join the DAV.

Now this is the good part. Terry was driving to his very first DAV meeting. It was hot, and he had the window down. Something happened, and he rolled his car over. His arm was out the window and got crushed. The doctors had to cut it off.

So, because he had a little hearing problem, he got into the DAV. And because he went to a DAV meeting, he ended up losing his arm. I know it's kinda sad him losing his arm and all, but it's kinda ironical too. I laughed when Terry told me that story. He told me he never thought about it that way, but then he laughed, too.

Most folks think he lost his arm in the war; you know, cause of all the DAV stuff he had. But Terry was my friend, so I know that wasn't so. He made me laugh. I miss him a lot.

70: Wilted

The Schreiendergeists followed a life path brightly illuminated by the burning bridges they had left behind. They were a couple who had yet to encounter a situation, product, or service that met with their satisfaction. The "Schreiendergeist experience" was enhanced by their belief that it was their obligation to inform every one of their shortcomings.

Consequently, there was not a doctor, lawyer, druggist, plumber, or random stranger within their community whom they hadn't "fired". When a need arose, they were forced to cast a wide net for assistance.

It came as a legitimate surprise when a gift was left on their doorstep: a beautiful, lush plant with no note or explanation. Mrs. Schreiendergeist was immediately captivated, an experience she briefly mistook for a mild stroke.

She found a home for the plant near the dining room, where it received abundant light. It flourished and produced delicate blue flowers that smelled of a tropical paradise.

The couple found pleasure in the plant. It brightened their mood, and they developed a disturbing sense of tolerance. They were even tempted to wave when a neighbor passed by.

Imperceptibly, they also began to change physically. Wrinkles softened, their bodies became toned, and their youthful hair color returned. Alarmingly, the age regression accelerated with time. Within a few weeks, the Schreiendergeists were giggling teenagers.

The neighbors noted an adolescent boy and girl elatedly playing in the Schreiendergeists' yard. The pleasant disposition of the children made it obvious that they were not related to the Schreiendergeists.

When approached, the young boy and girl were exceedingly polite and friendly, but were unable to give a satisfactory explanation for who they were or how they came to be in the Schreiendergeists' yard.

Chillingly, the Schreiendergeists themselves had completely vanished. The mystery of their disappearance remains unexplained to this day, though truthfully, it is not lamented.

A search for reports of missing children matching the description of the young boy and girl was fruitless. In time, they were taken into foster care by a gentle, childless couple and provided with a loving home.

Oddly, the children became increasingly sullen the longer they were away from the Schreiendergeist house and the beautiful plant. Though it broke their hearts, their foster parents found that they were unable to tolerate them. The boy and girl were separated and passed from foster home to foster home, leaving only a trail of wilted goodwill and bitter memories behind.

71: The Session

The author was invited to discuss his short story at a well-respected university writers' workshop. For nearly thirty years, his 293-word tale had been read, debated, and misunderstood in high schools, colleges, and graduate programs. While some praised it as bold, thought-provoking, and edgy, others found fault in the vague characters and ambiguous plot. He was well aware that this invitation could be a carefully staged ambush. Likewise, he had become adept at turning the hunter into the prey.

The opening salvo was polite, with a few curious questions about his choices for length, character development, and narrative pacing. But soon, the participants began circling, probing first with literary daggers, then with darts, and finally slinging arrows at the vague setting, the ambiguity of genders and nationalities, and the abrupt, inconclusive ending.

Throughout, the author remained pleasant, nodding thoughtfully, jotting down notes on a yellow legal pad. When the room quieted, he raised the yellow pad over his head.

"These are your thoughts on my story," he said. "Now I challenge you to take these insights and use them to improve it. I'll give you one hour. Your only constraint is to stay within my original word count."

He handed the legal pad to one of the participants and departed for a nearby lounge.

After an hour, he returned to a scene of chaos. The group had splintered into three separate factions. There was no consensus, and not a single rewritten story.

"I'll give you a little more time," he calmly offered. "Now combine the story and your critiques to create something better."

He returned to the lounge. He sipped a cup of coffee and enjoyed perusing the articles in a five-year-old magazine. Eventually, a participant came to retrieve him.

"We couldn't do it within the limitations you set," someone admitted. "The word count is too restrictive to develop the characters and plot fully."

"Are you saying that my story is flawed?" the author asked. "Only because it obeys limits?"

"No," someone else interjected, "We're saying the limits themselves are flawed."

The author reflected, "I crafted a tiny boat in a bottle. For thirty years, critics have lamented that my boat lacked detail, but this is the first time anyone has objected to the size of the bottle that I chose."

He nodded to no one in particular and quietly departed—unimpressed.

72: A Toast

The wedding rehearsal dinner had gone smoothly. After the meal was served, champagne was poured, and the groom's father stood to offer a toast. It was his nature to speak spontaneously and not to practice what he planned to say. He would regret that. Shortly into his toast, he was overcome with emotion and began sobbing. He could hardly get the words out. The message he had hoped to convey was unintelligible.

In the days that followed, he reflected on what he had meant to share.

"My father died when I was young, and we never really talked about love or marriage. However, I do recall an incident that gives me a clear sense of his views. I was probably about 10 years old, riding home from a wedding in the back seat of the car, with my mom and Dad in the front. My dad didn't think much of the bride. He and my mom were having a lively conversation about the poor choice they thought the groom had made.

"As they talked, my father laid out what he believed were the most important qualities in a bride. He valued both inner and outer beauty, maturity, intelligence, kindness, and—most importantly—that she loved the groom as much as he loved her.

"My dad was fortunate enough to have found such a woman. I did too. And now, so have each of my sons. Raise your glasses to the bride and groom. Son, you are a fortunate man."

Where did the tears come from? First, there was the memory of a trivial experience from long ago—of lost youth and long-gone parents. It was an event that had meant nothing to him at the time, but now it was a moment he longed to recapture. Who wouldn't want to be ten years old again? Who wouldn't give anything to share a few moments with their long-deceased parents? Not deep conversations—just the simple, relaxed interactions that we all once took for granted.

Then there was the realization that he had never shared these feelings with his wife of nearly forty years. Did she know how beautiful, intelligent, kind, and loving he found her to be? As a husband, he had not been demonstrative or even talkative about such things. He suddenly appreciated how unfair that had been to her. More importantly, in this regard, he realized he had set a poor example for his sons.

He could have practiced and delivered the toast exactly as he'd envisioned it. But as a son, as a husband, and as a father, he was glad to have experienced those emotions. Through those tears, he saw clearly what was important to him.

The father resolved to share this insight with his wife and sons the next time they were all gathered together.

Sadly, that moment would not come until his funeral.

73: Snow Day

He had just settled in with some cocoa after shoveling the walks when a loud knock hit the front door.

"We need a sixth player for Packers vs. Bears," John announced.

Steve threw his coat back on and buckled up his boots. Ten inches of powdery snow covered the ground. School had been canceled, so a neighborhood football game was the perfect idea.

The guys were all between ten and twelve, except for John's little brother David, who was six. Davey was pretty good at rushing the passer, and they bent the rules to allow him just to wrap someone up rather than tackle them to the ground. Otherwise, a good hard hit in the deep snow—with the thick coats, gloves, and hats—was what made the game so much fun. No one gave a second thought to tackling Allyson, aka Al; she was just one of the guys.

They gathered in the vacant lot by the widow Johnson's house and picked sides. As required by neighborhood rules, one team was always the Packers and the other was the Bears. Steve had once suggested Nebraska and Oklahoma, but no one other than Steve wanted to be stuck on the Nebraska side. They picked out trees to define out-of-bounds and drew lines in the snow with their boots to represent the goal lines. Rock-paper-scissors determined the receiving team.

The six-inch rubber football was punted to Al, who took off for the right sideline. John hit her at full speed (that is, full speed for an eleven-year-old wearing heavy winter clothes and running in ten inches of snow). They dropped in a clump, and Davey piled on. Steve took the position of quarterback; Al ran a slant, and Willie ran a comeback pattern. Davey counted to one thousand three and rushed the QB. Steve's pass floated into Willie's gloves over Tony's diving body. Willie spiked the ball in the end zone and did his stupid little dance. Packers 6, Bears 0.

After an hour and a half of non-stop running, everyone was sweaty under their coats. Their rapid breaths misted in the frigid air. The snow was packed down into a slick crust over most of the field. The score was Packers 96, Bears 84. Everyone had scored—even Davey. No one wanted to admit that their fingers and toes were getting cold. Mercifully, John and Davey's mom called them in for lunch.

Surprisingly, not one of the guys grew up to be a professional athlete. Every single one of them would try to introduce their own kids to Packers vs. Bears when the snow was deep enough. However, *Madden NFL* would inevitably win out. Kids nowadays need to touch grass (or snow).

74: The Odor

It was neither a pleasant nor an offensive smell, but it was pungent. The onset was sudden, and it deeply disturbed Tabby. It emanated from her, but she could not detect the exact location or a possible source. She soaked in a tub with an eucalyptus-scented bath bomb. Then she washed her hair with an organic, clarifying citrus shampoo. The fragrance was unchanged. She would have to remain isolated in her apartment until the air cleared. Thankfully, she could work from home.

Three days passed, and the boredom was driving her up the walls. She had to get out. A day at the beach would help to clear her mind. She found an empty stretch of Florida sand and laid out her blanket and tote bag. The mango-scented sunscreen did little to mask her intimate aroma. She did take solace in the fact that no one was close enough to notice.

In the distance, a family with two young children played carefree in the surf. The soothing rhythm of the waves allowed her to relax and give serious consideration to what her next course of action should be. She realized that time alone was not going to resolve the issue. Likewise, superficial cleansing and aromatic products were not the solution. She would have to seek professional consultation.

Heads turned when she entered her doctor's office. The time spent with the receptionist was brief, and Tabby was briskly shown back to an exam room, and the door closed. The doctor recoiled slightly as he entered. She explained the sudden onset of the smell and the failure of her previous efforts to overcome it. The doctor questioned her about changes in diet, medication, clothing, pets, furnishings, and household or personal care products. Nothing was new or different. The doctor carefully examined Tabby and found no evidence of any physical ailment. He ordered an array of screening labs and scans.

She returned home and once again to the tedium of isolation. Tabby was catching up on past issues of a news magazine when she noticed that a prisoner had been executed in Texas. She recognized the name. The memories were suddenly fresh.

Twelve years ago, she had served on the jury that found him guilty. She had been one of two holdouts against conviction. In her mind, there was reasonable doubt, but she had acquiesced to pressure and changed her vote. She had moved on and had not thought about it since then.

The article detailed how the condemned prisoner had steadfastly maintained his innocence throughout the arduous appeals process. His last words sent a chill down her spine.

"My death is cloaked in the stench of injustice."

She suddenly regretted changing her vote. Just as suddenly, her cynical subconscious questioned whether her remorse was due to the death of an innocent man—or to being cursed with an odor.

The answer was obvious.

75: The Table

The table had once been the center of a family. Four, six, and sometimes eight people had gathered around it to celebrate birthdays, Easter, Thanksgiving, and Christmas.

A lonely, frightened young woman rested her elbows on the table, praying for her soldier husband. The warm, soft glow of candles reflected off it for their romantic dinner when he returned.

A bassinet sat on it for the baby's first bite of solid food. Later, it bore the crumbs, spills, and mess from countless meals fed to a small army of children.

Children had colored and done their homework on its surface. It was the same surface that had been marred by paint, knives, and even hammers when they had a "project."

It transformed into a desk for bill paying and the dreaded yearly ritual of filling out income tax forms. Christmas cards began their journey there, and so did epic games of Monopoly.

The grain of the wood absorbed the oils as Grandma rolled out the dough and the grandkids cut out Christmas cookies. This was followed by decorating and yet another spectacular mess.

The table solemnly bore the cluster of casseroles, sandwiches, bars, cookies, and brownies that arrived after Grandpa died. Then it supported the widow as she read through the sympathy cards and wrote out her thank-you notes.

Finally, it was this table that became a work surface for closing up the family home. Boxes were placed on it and filled with all the contents of drawers, cupboards, and closets. It was the last piece of furniture removed from the home. The house was empty.

The table now sat alone in a used furniture shop—homeless, abandoned. Why? How could something so intimately woven into a family's life be cast aside?

76: A Dreamer

The evolution was so slow and stealthy that no one realized what had happened. The ways of the past just faded from memory. The new reality became the norm.

There was no religion. Everyone lived for today. Countries, nationalities, and possessions disappeared. There was nothing to kill or die for. The world lived in peace. There was no greed or hunger, only the brotherhood of man. The dream had come true. All the world was one.

John Lennon was forgotten, but had he been remembered, this might have seemed familiar.

The only remaining vestige of the old way was the World Crisis Organization. It was a group dedicated to the misdiagnosis of crises in the world, bringing inordinate attention to them, and applying inappropriate or tyrannical solutions to them. Or at least, that's how they were viewed by the current mainstream media.

The annual WCO meeting in Stockholm was poorly attended, and those members present were in poor spirits. These were men and women who had worked fervently their entire lives to bring light to the existential crises that threatened the existence of mankind. Now, everyone lived tranquilly with not a care in the world. This "brotherhood of man" and "all the world is one" delusion had taken the wind out of their sails.

Discussions centered on how to regain momentum. What injustice, what potential calamity, could they now identify and promote? When there is no Heaven or Hell, social injustice becomes more difficult to define and market. Likewise, environmental issues are less urgent when the populace lives for today in peace and harmony. The elimination of possessions, greed, and hunger was a roadblock to the tried-and-true humanitarian campaigns.

Three separate points of view emerged. Some felt that they should be self-congratulatory regarding having done so well in solving the world's problems. Others felt the organization had become irrelevant and should disband. And finally, some felt that new crises would arise and the WCO needed to remain vigilant to recognize and deal with them as needed. The loyalists pledged to gather again next year in Geneva.

Unspoken was the concept that humanity needs a crisis to remain vital. A secretive core group planned to "initiate" a crisis to make certain that the Geneva meeting was more "productive".

77: Blank

He sat with his back to the wall, staring out the window. The silence unnerved him.

"Just put some words down. You can rearrange them later," he begged himself.

Nothing. He got up and stepped outside, hoping the world might offer inspiration. But everything felt dull, lifeless. The sky hung low, the clouds motionless. Even the wind seemed indifferent.

"What had happened to him?" Words were the raw material of his craft, yet he couldn't even string three or four together. His thoughts were tangled, nonsensical, and useless.

The critics were right. He was overthinking it, trying too hard. He needed to relax and just let the process happen.

"But what does that even mean?"

He had been patient too long, waiting for an idea that never came. Now he was under the gun. There were just two days before the event. His reputation and legacy were on the line.

"For God's sake, man, you're the State Poet Laureate," he told himself bitterly.

For sixty years, he had written about the prairie, the Indigenous people, corn, cattle, the Platte River, tornadoes, sod houses, buffalo, the Unicameral, dust storms, the Cornhuskers, the Union Pacific Railroad—the whole damn state.

It was all there, buried in his past work. He just needed to dig something up and rework it. No one ever paid attention anyway. No problem—he would find something obscure.

He laughed cynically at the thought. In this day and age, *all poetry is obscure.* He realized that his life's work had become irrelevant. No one appreciated poetry anymore.

That was something he could work with—an *art form in search of an audience.* The contemporary *silencing of the music of the written word* was insidious. The juices were flowing now. Words were finding a place in the framework he was constructing.

This is what he did.

He was a poet.

78: The Destination

The husband and wife worked seamlessly together organizing for the trip and loading the car. The harmony hit a sour note as soon as they got inside. As usual, he plugged their destination into the GPS. Meanwhile, she spread out a large map, covering the passenger side of the vehicle.

"I don't know why you even mess with that thing. Don't you want to know the route that we'll be traveling? There might be things we want to stop and see."

"Right, and there might be road construction or traffic accidents that your map doesn't show—but my GPS does."

And they were off. For the first hour, things went smoothly. They found a station on Sirius XM that they both liked and even had some pleasant conversation. Then the inevitable happened.

"The map shows we should take I-29 South here to pick up Highway 92 East."

"The GPS has me continuing north on I-80."

"That takes you way out of the way north."

"It may be a little further, but the interstate is 70-MPH and a decent road. Highway 92 is two-lane, slower, and goes through small towns."

"You're being ridiculous. I'm sure it's just as fast, and you get to see something other than exit signs, overpasses, and medians."

Map vs. GPS, the never-ending story. He deemed GPS navigation the greatest invention of his lifetime. She preferred the rich elegance and explicit details of the cartographer's art.

"Why are you exiting here?"

"The GPS shows some sort of bottleneck with traffic backed up. It is directing us around it. Something your map can't do."

"This doesn't look right. You're heading into a state park."

"I'm just following directions. I'm sure it has a reason to take us this way."

"Stop following the GPS and look at your surroundings. Whoa, whoa! You're heading down a boat ramp! Stop!"

"Whoops," he said sheepishly, realizing there was no graceful way to explain away the lake staring them in the face.

"I swear, you never listen to me. You trust that stupid technology more than you trust me," her voice cracked. "That thing is useless. If you had taken Highway 92 like I tried to tell you, we'd probably be there now.”

"OK, OK, get me out of here," he replied softly.

She studied her map.

GPS: *Recalculating*

79: Change

They stood by the sink, washing and drying dishes—a nightly ritual that had long ago lost its romantic charm. He embraced innovation and technology. She valued simplicity and tradition. It wasn't that he was lazy. He just thought a dishwasher would do a better job of cleaning the dishes. They needed to get with the times.

She flatly refused. They didn't need a dishwasher.

He argued that they could comfortably afford it. He even offered to give her a dishwasher for her birthday or Christmas. She countered that it wasn't the expense; it was simply that they did not need a dishwasher.

They went back and forth for months. Each night, he silently chafed at what he saw as a needless chore. She continued, content to do things just as her grandmother and great-grandmother had.

Inspiration came to him one morning while shaving. If he couldn't give her a dishwasher, she would have to *win* one.

He bought a roll of professional-looking raffle tickets at Office Depot. A wiry neighborhood boy with a fondness for mischief was enlisted. The boy would approach his wife and sell her a raffle ticket for the "Booster Club". She was an easy mark for the town's frequent fundraisers, and his scheme worked perfectly. After thirty days, he sent the boy back to announce to his wife that she had won the raffle.

"Really, what did I win?"

"A brand-new, deluxe dishwasher," the boy replied enthusiastically. "When would you like to have it delivered?"

"That's such a nice prize," was her polite response. "But we don't need a dishwasher. Draw another ticket and give it to someone who can use it."

80: Insight

Lester and I are living the dream. We're both fortunate to have union pensions, Social Security, and the bonus that all of our ex-wives are remarried. Our retirement involves spending leisurely afternoons at the Lazy Leprechaun Lounge over a pitcher or two of beer. A while back, our friend Stretch got up and began singing a Christmas tune. It was closer to the 4th of July than to Christmas, but Stretch has a good voice, and we just kind of let him go with it.

Forgive me, I mention this only because it got me thinking about Santa Claus. Suddenly, I put it all together—well, Lester helped a little too.

First of all, Santa Claus is real. Here's the kicker: there are a lot of them. Now I can't speak for the entire world, but here in the good old US of A, there are thousands of them. And they're all in the witness relocation program.

Here's how it works: the cops pick up a guy breaking and entering. He's not a dangerous, murderous type. Just a thief who's good at breaking into homes. Now they offer him a chance to go to work for them. The witness protection people relocate him to a north-of-nowhere town and give him a new identity, house, and a decent job. All he has to do is sneak around and deliver presents on Christmas Eve each year. As long as he doesn't return to his previous criminal proclivities, everything is hunky-dory.

Here's Lester's input: the toys are all donated. You know the toy drives run by the Marines, the Salvation Army, and others? Well, those toys are stockpiled all over the country. Then, on Christmas Eve, the Santas distribute them.

There you have it. No North Pole, no elves, no sleigh or reindeer; just a bunch of ex-criminals running around, breaking into houses and leaving gifts. I know this to be absolutely true. Because I'm a union member from New Jersey, and I know people who know people.

81: Yesterday

The Eagles' *Peaceful Easy* Feeling softly hovered in the air. Cocoa butter-scented candles surrounded the tub in a dimly lit room. Jill sank into the luxuriant bubbles floating over the warm water and closed her eyes.

The scent, the song, the tranquility gently pulled her mind back to the lake.

She laid her towel out on the beach at Logan Lake and applied Coppertone Cocoa Butter to her arms and legs. Suzy helped with her back. Her favorite Jantzen kelly-green bikini covered just enough to pass her mom's modesty inspection. She positioned herself on her front and gazed out at the water through her oversized, round Givenchy sunglasses. Suzy and Bett lay on towels beside her. A group of boys were having chicken fights in the water. The girls giggled when Sam took a header.

The sun felt good on her skin, and she rolled over on her back to even out her tan. She liked the song on the radio and leaned over to turn it up. She could no longer see the guys, but Suzy and Bett provided a vivid commentary. Suddenly, they were excited—the boys were coming out of the water and approaching them. She sat up.

She opened her eyes in the present and looked down. The parting bubbles revealed sagging breasts and a belly roll. She smiled. She had had some very good yesterdays.

****

Sam grabbed a new bar of soap and headed into the shower. As he lathered up, he detected the distinct aroma of cocoa butter. The scent brought back memories of those times at Logan Lake. The guys were buff, and the girls were hot. It never entered his mind that he wouldn't be able to keep that body forever. He remembered how good Jill had looked in that bright green bikini and how relentlessly he had tried to impress her. She had been his crush all summer. He had been frustrated trying to separate her from Bett and Suzy. It was a mystery why guys could fly solo, but girls always seemed to fly in formation. The recollections aroused him, but when he looked down, there was no visible evidence of it.

Those were good times. He wondered what had become of Jill. Did she ever think of him?

He rinsed and toweled off. He caught a glimpse of a seventy-ish naked man in the mirror and smiled.

"Whoa," he murmured. "Glad Jill can't see me now."

82: Silently

It began innocently with a bologna sandwich in the faculty lounge—why not *bolona sanwich*? The professor quietly wondered if English might be better off without silent letters. He noted that they confuse non-English speakers trying to learn the language and also complicate spelling for native speakers. It became his mission to make the language more intuitive, easier to read, and easier to learn.

First, he needed to identify the letters that were silent in English words. After careful study, he determined that all the letters in the alphabet could be silent except for F, J, Q, R, and V. He determined that some accommodation had to be made for the spelling of words with different meanings, but the same pronunciation. Maybe it would work to substitute the letter V for all the silent letters. Then musically would become *musicvly*, or climb would become *climv*, or muscle would become *musvlv*. That was an improvement, but still not quite what he was looking for.

Next, he tried leaving out all the silent letters unless they were needed to differentiate the identically pronounced words. If he used the universal V substitute, the sentence "Pick up four sandwiches and an almond cake next Wednesday at the Gnarly Knob Bakery for school," would become, "*Pik* up *fovr sanwiches* and an *amond cak* next *Wensda* at the *Narly Nob* Bakery for *scool*." It was much better, but not yet perfect.

He could see that some silent letters affected the pronunciation of preceding vowels, such as the O in close or the A in day. It was probably best to leave the silent E or Y alone.

But other silent letters like G, K, P, and T didn't seem to have that property. In that case, "He scratched his knee on the cupboard door while designing a sign on butcher paper for the raspberry patch," would become, "He *scrached* his *nee* on the *cuboard* door while *desining* a *sin* on *bucher* paper for the *rasberry pach*." Again, it was much better, but still not perfect.

Maybe he should throw in the universal V for each silent G, K, P, and T. Then we would have, "He *scravched* his *vnee* on the *cuvboard* door while *desivning* a *sivn* on *buvcher* paper for the *rasvberry pavch*." Now that was perfect, the worthless silent G, K, P, and T replaced with the universal silent V. He couldn't wait to share his research with his colleagues.

He published his work in a prestigious academic journal to rave reviews. Naturally, he applied for a government grant to fund further research, the development of a revised dictionary, and a plan for a nationwide re-education program. Three graduate assistants were recruited, and supercomputer time was requested. The project was expected to take five years.

Unfortunately, the journal article came to the attention of the American Academy of Scrabble Aficionados. Their political action arm brought pressure to bear on narrow-minded politicians. The resulting uproar led to the denial of his grant application.

To this day, the English language remains difficult to learn and spell. However, the professor refused to abandon his dream. He left the Vsychology Department at Vnucklehead University and moved to Champaivn, Illinois, to engage in vsychic research on gvosts and wivches.

83: Emily

Little Emily, delicate in her blue dress and white socks, sat on a folding chair between two aunts. Just three-years-old, she clutched a small stuffed squirrel, her legs swinging gently beneath her seat.

The Pastor entered the room, his white robes flowing, a purple stole draped over his shoulders, and a silver cross resting on his chest. His warm gaze lingered on little Emily before he turned to address the group, "I'd like to pray with you before we enter the Sanctuary for the funeral service, but first, please allow me a moment with Emily."

He knelt in front of Emily and met her gaze. He spoke slowly and softly. "Emily, do you know what a soul is?"

She shook her head, eyes downcast, clutching her stuffed animal.

"Well, your soul is the part of you that never changes, even when you grow up. It's the part that loves, the part that laughs, the part that feels warm when someone hugs you. Do you think that part ever goes away?"

Emily, now looking up, shook her head gently from side to side.

"I don't think so either. I like to think our souls are like candles that still keep burning even when we leave a room. The flame just keeps burning. What do you think?"

She held her squirrel up, "Stuffy doesn't go away, even when I close my eyes."

The Pastor smiled warmly, "That's absolutely right. And it feels good to know your stuffy is still there even when you can't see him, doesn't it?"

She nodded, and her eyes brightened.

"I believe our souls are always with God. The part of your mommy and daddy that made you laugh, that hugged you, and that loved you didn't go away even though you can't see them anymore."

Emily loosened her grip, nodded, and smiled sweetly.

As he rose, there were a few quiet sighs, a soft rustle of tissues. He turned to the family and gently said, "Please bow your heads and join me in prayer… for love that never fades, for souls that live on forever with our Heavenly Father…"

84: Class of '69

They had so much fun together. Fifty-some years of adventure. Now it was winding down. Her pancreatic cancer diagnosis was a wake-up call to reality. She had decided to forego the surgery and chemo and just let nature take its course. He, of course, didn't agree, but respected her right to make that decision. She chose to live the time she had left to the fullest. And that's why the ad caught his eye.

He couldn't have afforded it when it first came out. The 1969 Mustang GT convertible had a 5.0L, 32-valve, 412 HP V8. Quad headlamps and aggressive stance made it stand out from previous models. It was a beauty to behold. Even the Acapulco Blue color with black vinyl interior was to his liking.

He remembered holding her hand as they admired a similar car in the dealer showroom while seniors in high school. He promised her that one day they would own that car. To his surprise, she remembered that moment too. It took no convincing to get her to sign on for one last great road trip. They would travel what remained of Route 66 in that car.

Ten days at a leisurely pace was the plan, depending, of course, on how comfortable she felt with the travel. They started in June at the "Begin Historic Route 66" sign, the top up and Chicago temperatures in the mid-60s. The car was a pure pleasure to drive, drawing admiring glances and waves as they cruised into the rural plains.

The top came down as they moved farther south into Missouri, and she sported a scarf over her hair. The journey became a moving celebration of their life together. They took every opportunity to stop at roadside attractions, especially ones with historical significance. Her energy was fading, but she never tired of shopping at the local venues. Her purse and the glove box overflowed with postcards and mementos.

They started the eighth day near Gallup, New Mexico, jumping back and forth between the original road and Interstate 40. On the old roadway, something unexpected happened. Suddenly, an approaching pickup truck made a left-hand turn right in front of them. He didn't even have time to hit the brakes. He just swerved hard to the left, squeezed his eyes shut, and braced for impact.

But there was no impact. Somehow, impossibly, they missed the truck completely. Neither one of them could believe it. It was a miracle.

As they continued down Route 66, they began to enjoy the perfect reproduction billboards from the 1960s. They saw the old brands and ad campaigns they remembered from their youth. He noticed that the cars seemed to be vintage from the fifties and sixties, too. He glanced over at her, and she looked just as beautiful as she had in high school. Her thick black hair flowed in the wind. She reached over and put her hand on his knee. He looked down, and his leg was muscular and tan.

"Honey, let's pull over here," she said, motioning to a fifties-style motor court. There was a seductive sweetness in her voice.

Blushing, he eased the car into the gravel parking lot. Holding hands, they walked into the motel office with a youthful bounce in their step.

85: A Poem

The dinner was casual, but some of the attendees were tense. The plates were cleared, and champagne was poured. Alice Hunklefort-Langley rose to address the gathering.

Alice had inherited both the family fortune and its commitment to supporting emerging writers. She still possessed the sharp intelligence that had made her a formidable literary critic in her youth. Age had softened her famous acerbic wit into something resembling kindness, yet her presence defined gravitas.

"I must congratulate all the participants in our 45th annual writers' workshop. The submissions were excellent, and the selection committee's decision was arduous. Please raise your glasses and toast this year's recipient of the Hunklefort Prize: C.K. Raintree for her untitled poem."

"Hear, hear," came the chorus from the guests as glasses were clinked.

The author, a slight woman in her forties, clothed in an eclectic bohemian style, rose from her chair. She spoke in a slow, deliberate voice.

Iowa

What?

Iowa

Where?

Iowa

When?

Iowa

Why?

Iowa

The group politely applauded. Some smiled, but many appeared perplexed.

The evening concluded with participants exchanging information and bidding each other goodbye. There were handshakes and promises to keep in touch.

Franklin approached the workshop director, Dr. Taylor.

"Excuse me, but I just have to say that I don't get anything out of that poem. What does it mean to you?"

"I see it as an exquisite use of free verse to stimulate each reader differently, causing them to probe their preconceived impressions for significance," the professor replied.

"But what does it stimulate in you, professor?"

"Personally, I struggle to imagine one entity as being the sum total of all the questions in life," he replied.

"So 'Iowa' is the answer to all the questions in life?"

"Franklin, Iowa, is a metaphor. C.K. is challenging each of us to find our own 'Iowa'."

"I respect your opinion, professor, but in my view, that's just overthinking a very bad poem.

It would have gotten a poor grade in most high school English classes."

"Ah, Franklin, if high school teachers understood poetry, we wouldn't need the writers' workshop, would we?"

86: The Dilemma

The answer shocked him. He shifted uncomfortably in his chair and instinctively broke eye contact to gaze down at the floor. He recognized instantly that he was confronted with an ethical dilemma. Professional confidentiality required that he not disclose what his patient had just told him. But someone else could be harmed. He had to seek the advice of his older partner.

"A patient revealed something to me that might be morally and legally wrong. Would I be violating confidentiality if I discussed it with you?" the young doctor asked.

"My view is that we can discuss a case provided you do not reveal the patient's identity," the older doctor replied. "Does this involve the potential for harm to another individual?"

"Possibly. The patient was vague, and I may be reading too much into what he said."

"Okay, do your suspicions rise to the level of a mandatory report?"

"Again, possibly. I hesitate because of the Henderson tragedy. That investigation ruined reputations and lives over allegations that later proved false. Once the hint of sexual scandal gets out, there is no going back."

"No social worker or peer review committee would consider that a valid reason for not reporting the possibility of abuse. You are putting your license at risk," his partner counseled.

"If I'm wrong, it could destroy a family."

"If you are right, there is a moral and professional obligation to protect innocent victims. Yes, we have seen an overzealous investigator whose techniques caused harm. However, at some point, you have to trust the professionalism of those who will do the inquiry."

"I just don't know that I can trust them. If I've misread what the patient said, I'm turning him into the victim."

"Well, you need to bring your patient back promptly and make certain that you clearly understand what was said." Then he added, "Sometimes, finding the right course of action, legally or ethically, takes time and thoughtful review. The sooner you make that determination, the better."

The older physician reflected on the idealism of his young partner. There had been no dilemma for him in the Henderson case. He seldom empathized. He was cynical. His knee-jerk response was to report the possibility of abuse and let the chips fall where they may. That cynicism had led him to report suspicions that Rachel Henderson was abusing her teenage son. An obsessive, self-righteous social worker had exposed Rachel to intense public humiliation. She was ultimately vindicated, but tragically not before her death.

He appreciated the diligence and compassion of his young partner. There was danger in the cautious approach, but he knew too well that nothing could undo the damage once a name was tainted or a life was lost.

87: Hoops

It was just a fluff human interest piece: five hundred words and a picture. A couple of women had played one-on-one basketball every Wednesday for twenty-five years. The two had become a minor legend at the local Y. She'd spend an hour tops with the interview and photo and have it on her editor's desk by noon. Truthfully, she already had it written in her head. She just needed a few specific details; otherwise, it was generic.

She arrived at the gym and approached the two women already engaged in a vigorous half-court game. One was Black, lean, and tall. The other was Hispanic, short, and muscular. Both appeared to be in their early forties. The shorter one drove in for a layup, which the taller one blocked. The shooter snapped up the rebound and made a slick spin-around jumper that saw nothing but net.

"Pegleg, still toooo tall and toooo slow," she taunted as her opponent returned the ball to mid-court. Her voice carried the self-assurance of someone who had perfected this particular insult long ago.

It was then that they noticed the reporter. She walked out onto the court and was immediately flustered. Watching them play, she had only seen two athletic women. Now she noticed that the tall woman's leg ended above the knee and was fitted with a metal prosthesis. The shorter player was sporting a prosthetic right arm below the shoulder.

"You must be Shaniqua and Carmella," she stuttered, her preplanned questions suddenly forgotten.

"In here, we're Lefty and Pegleg," Shaniqua countered, dribbling between her legs with casual skill. "Keeps things simple."

The reporter fumbled for her notebook, trying to recover her professional footing. "OK, I understand you've been playing each other a long time. How did that start?"

"Peg here was having trouble adjusting to her disability; you know, kind of depressed. The occupational therapist told her that several handicapped kids were working out at the YMCA. He introduced us and we clicked," Lefty volunteered.

The reporter chose her response carefully and delivered it in a well-practiced, sensitive tone. "Some people might find the terms 'disability' and 'handicapped' offensive or hurtful."

"Ever heard of the Americans with *Disabilities* Act or *Disabled* American Veterans? How about *handicapped* parking spaces? What is really offensive and hurtful is when people get all sensitive around us," Pegleg shot back, her voice resolute. "Treat us and talk to us just like you would anyone else. You can't create words or phrases to soften what is obvious. We are not like you. We know it. Acknowledge it and move on."

"Did you come here to write about a basketball rivalry or about societal inadequacies? Take a picture of me leaving the one-legged Amazon, stuck in her tracks," Lefty said as she faked right, then swept left past Pegleg and headed for the basket.

They were right, of course. They deserved to be seen for who they were—the two women she saw when she first walked into the gym— athletes bound by friendship and love of the game. The story wrote itself.

88: Ants

She awoke to a tickling sensation in her nose. Half-awake, she reached up to brush away what she assumed was a strand of hair. It was an ant, and others were crawling on her face. She sat up to find dozens of ants on the sheets.

She had left the bedroom window open a crack to let the night air in. The ants had taken advantage of the breach. She quickly closed the window and noted the thick cloud of flying ants in the yard. They seemed to be everywhere, a literal invasion.

Her house was like a leaking boat in a sea of ants. Meticulously, she sealed window sills and door thresholds with duct tape. The vacuum cleaner made quick work of the larger congregations of ants, but there were still a few—here, there, and everywhere.

They crawled up her leg. They floated in the milk on her cereal. The little buggers were even on her toothbrush. This was war. She became possessed, driven by rage and revulsion.

Desperate times call for strategic thinking. She set out bowls of maple syrup to attract them, which worked quite well. Still, a few pesky ones resisted the bait.

Cupboards were emptied and vacuumed, but they were reinvaded as soon as the contents were replaced.

Duct tape became her secret weapon, repurposed as flypaper. The sticky barriers were only temporary, as the hordes crawled over the entrapped bodies of their fallen comrades.

There was a bug zapper sitting tantalizingly close on the back patio, but she was not about to open the door to go get it.

She found an old can of pesticide and sprayed a few areas. Although effective, the noxious fumes were enough to convince her this wasn't her best option.

Vacuum cleaner hose in hand, she established a citadel on a swivel chair in the middle of the living room. Any ant that approached was swiftly dispensed with. This had become a siege. She had to concede that she could not defend her entire home, but she certainly would defend her personal space. None shall pass.

The day gave way to night. She had gone without food or drink since taking her place on the swivel-chair citadel. Even so, the call of nature required that she retreat to the bathroom. The ants seemed fewer in number and less aggressive, but she sensed it was only a ruse.

After taking care of business, she assessed her bedroom. She convinced herself that the situation was manageable and moved her bowls of syrup and vacuum cleaner to the bedroom. She closed the door and duct-taped the threshold. The sheets and pillows were thoroughly vacuumed and inspected. One final perimeter sweep, then she lay down and fell into a deep sleep.

Daylight streamed into the room as she awoke to a tickling sensation in her nose and on her lips. Once more, she girded for battle.

89: Lost Dutchman

Craggy, weathered, and used up, he had endured the worst the desert could do to a man. At eighty-three, by his best guess, there wasn't much left of him. It was difficult to walk over the uneven ground. A fall would most likely fracture a hip, and he would lie there as nature took its course. He didn't care. He would make his way back to Wickenburg one last time or die trying. He was out of provisions, had a toothache, and his boots needed repair.

A man, a mule, and a mutt: they were interdependent and inseparable. They had thrived in the desert against all odds. The man was the only original member of the team. There had been another mule and four other dogs. He had purposely named each mule Abe and every dog Wilson to make them easy to remember.

They had never found the *Lost Dutchman Mine*. Long ago, he had concluded that it was just a myth used to sell maps. He had found some copper, silver, and a little gold in his time. Though never rich, he survived. That was all he could expect to do.

He had taken to the desert forty years ago after a divorce. She was probably dead by now. There was some kindness in his life when he was with her. He had treated her badly and run away from the shame of his failure. The search for gold was just an excuse not to return to the world of a job, family, and home. It was six to nine months of prospecting, followed by a week or so in "civilization".

He knew he was not a good man. He had killed at least two men and possibly a third. That was the way of the desert. You could never relax. If nature didn't get you, bad men would. These men had attacked him for his meager possessions and had learned that they were messing with the wrong Marine. He was smart enough to leave no evidence of foul play. When their skeletal remains were discovered, it would appear that the desert had just claimed another inexperienced hiker. Still, the guilt lingered. Soon enough, he would answer for his sins.

Wilson and Abe were his only friends. He had learned to eat and drink what the desert provided when his provisions ran low. He bore the heat and bundled up for the cold. He knew that the desert only tolerated him and could dispose of him without warning. He'd probably long overstayed his welcome.

The desert was changing in ways that he didn't like. Idiots on machines ran wild in a cloud of dust and intolerable noise. Ten years ago—no, twenty—he would have carried out guerrilla warfare against them. Now he could only impotently curse them.

What did he have to show for his nine decades? Nothing tangible, no family, no friends. Just a mule and a dog. He asked himself: Do you want to die in a bed or a bedroll?

The tooth wasn't bothering him that much, and he'd make do with his boots. There was nothing in Wickenburg for him anymore—no friends, no memories worth reclaiming.

He looked at his bedroll strapped to Abe and turned around. The sun was behind him now. He would head for Sayer Spring first. Then, Lord willing, he'd make his way to Sam Powell Peak.

90: Karen

The rental car crept along at barely five miles per hour. With the celebrity home map on her lap and both their heads on a swivel, they gawked at the luxurious homes.

"I'm pretty sure a couple of the names on this map are dead," he said.

"Oh, look on the left. That's Lucy and Desi's house," she exclaimed.

"Divorced and dead," was his disgusted reply.

"OK, but that's where they used to live. Honestly, I thought it would be bigger."

Neither of them saw Karen, a lean blonde in her mid-40s, jogging on the left side of the road. Suddenly, she made a sharp left turn and purposely ran into the left front fender of the car. The impact knocked her to the ground, where she sprawled dramatically onto the pavement, feigning loss of consciousness.

He slammed on the brakes, and they both jumped out to check on the victim. She dialed 911 while he checked the jogger for breathing and a pulse.

"Is she dead?" she asked sheepishly.

"No, just unconscious, I think. Does she look familiar to you? Kind of like that actress from *The Hunger Games*." He replied, his voice a mixture of concern and puzzlement.

"That is not Jennifer Garner," she shot back.

"Honey, Jennifer Garner wasn't even in *Hunger Games*. That was Jennifer Lawrence, but I'm thinking of the one with the funny hair." He offered, partially connecting the dots.

"I know who you mean, but I think it's that comedian who looks like her. You know the one with the talk show that Gladys thinks is so obnoxious."

"Yeah, I think you're right—Chelsea, something," he concluded, proud of having solved the puzzle.

With sirens blaring and lights flashing, the EMTs arrived. They quickly assessed the victim, who had *"regained consciousness."*

"Can you tell me your name and where you are?" one of the EMTs asked.

"Karen Schultz. I was jogging down Roxbury Drive before that car ran me down."

Her heart sank, "Not Chelsea what's-her-name, but a complete nobody."

"Wait a minute. She ran into me!" he exclaimed, suddenly back in touch with reality and the seriousness of the situation.

"Calm down. The cops will be here in a few minutes and take your statement. Whatever happened, there are more surveillance cameras per square foot here than anywhere else on the planet. If it's not your fault, you have nothing to worry about."

"Just our luck," she thought. "We ran over someone in Beverly Hills, and they're not even a celebrity! What are the odds?"

Alert and acutely aware of the conversation about video evidence, Karen came to grips with her situation. "Damn my luck," she thought. "How could I be so stupid as to try to pull this scam here? If I'd stayed in Fresno, I'd be halfway to a settlement by now."

91: Primghar

The Primgharians are a strange-looking lot. The Primgharians' appearance—a result of generations of intermarriage—startled the Portuguese sailors who first charted the island in the early 1600s. Its isolation in the South Pacific had allowed the small native population to live undisturbed, up until that time.

Primgharians seem otherworldly—small in stature, with no discernible chin and a high-pitched nasal voice. So much so, in fact, that a recent TV program made the case that they were the descendants of "ancient aliens."

However, modern geneticists speculate that centuries ago, a single individual with a condition known as micrognathia was introduced into the population. Generations of secluded intermarriage made the trait universal.

What modern science cannot explain is how the Primgharians communicate. Some say they didn't speak at all, only watched and smiled, as if they already knew the outcome of every conversation. Though they possess a spoken language, they can also read each other's minds. Even more remarkable is that they can also read the thoughts of outsiders.

As a few of the Primgharians learned Spanish, the Spaniards noted that the little fellows seemed to be able to anticipate their actions. This trait made Primgharians invaluable in diplomatic situations, and utterly terrifying in personal encounters. Understandably, the Spaniards quickly moved to exploit this advantage.

The Primgharian crisis began when a few Primgharians were taken to Spain. There, they were placed in intensive language programs to learn English, French, German, Italian, Dutch, or Russian. Soon, Spanish envoys were routinely accompanied by the exotic "personal secretaries," who lacked a chin. For a few years, Spanish interests flourished.

It did not take long for the secret to be discovered. All the major nations began to employ their own Primgharians. Smaller nations began to fear a perceived Primgharian gap. The concern over Primgharian proliferation resulted in the *Strategic Primgharian Limitation Treaty.*

Enforcing the treaty proved to be impossible. The tactical advantage of employing Primgharians was lost when nearly everyone had one. Additionally, world leaders became increasingly paranoid that Primgharians might disclose their thoughts to the people they governed.

Eventually, nations stockpiled a Primgharian or two—just in case. Otherwise, they reverted to conventional diplomacy. However, the covert use of Primgharians remains an omnipresent threat against enemies, foreign and domestic.

The Primgharians themselves detest this international intrigue. They prefer to live a peaceful life on their island, as their ancestors had done for generations. The beautiful island of Primghar remains a remote destination for the wealthy and adventurous. It is said that no reservations are required. They know you are coming.

92: Doubt

He was nearly paralyzed by his fear. Sweat beaded up on his brow, his hands trembled, and he had difficulty concentrating. He stood before the sink and forced himself to scrub. Silently, he begged God to get him through this: "Don't let me screw this up." Then he immediately regretted the selfish nature of his prayer and contritely asked for the success of the surgery and the recovery of the patient.

He stepped into the OR, and the scrub nurse handed him a towel. He dried his hands and she helped him gown and glove. Together, they prepped and draped the patient. This was it; he was now deep in concentration on the task before him. Fear and apprehension disappeared.

"We good?" he asked, looking toward the anesthetist.

"O2 sat is good; pulse and BP are stable," was the reply.

He made the standard laparotomy incision through the skin and underlying tissues. The scrub suctioned and sponged as he tied and cauterized bleeders. He elevated and opened the peritoneum. Retractors were placed, and he breathed a sigh of relief when there was no evidence of massive hemorrhage in the abdominal cavity. Maybe the bullet had missed the major organs and vessels. The preoperative exam had revealed a single gunshot entrance wound to the right of the abdominal midline and an exit wound in the left flank. He examined the stomach, liver, spleen, kidneys, and aorta. He ran the bowel, looking for holes. He counted eight and repaired them. There was a small nick in a mesenteric artery; he repaired that also. He looked for any evidence of clothing or debris along the bullet tract and removed a small cloth fragment. He irrigated the cavity with saline and an antibiotic solution.

He stood over the patient and looked carefully for any evidence of active bleeding. Convinced that the field was dry, they did a sponge and needle count, and he closed the surgical incision in layers. An ABD pad was applied. The bullet wounds were cleaned and bandaged but not sutured.

"OK for me to go face the family?" he asked the anesthetist, who nodded OK.

The mother sat stoically in a private area. He knelt beside her and gently held her hands as he told her that the surgery had gone well. He reassured her that her son's prognosis was good. She looked up at him with relief and thanked him profusely.

Heart pounding, he gasped as he awoke. The dream was always the same. He was cursed to vividly see the trust in her eyes and hear the hope in her voice every night.

A hunting accident in a remote area presented unique challenges. Transfer to another facility or surgeon was not a realistic option. He had done his best, but still failed.

In the early post-operative period, he failed to recognize the signs of traumatic pancreatitis. The subsequent death of the boy shattered his confidence. If he had transferred his patient, once stable, to another facility, things might have turned out differently. But he didn't.

He was consumed with remorse. Deep inside, every surgeon knows the feeling. There is an old medical adage: *A chance to cut is a chance to cure… or cry.* Even the best surgeons encounter complications. It is a statistical certainty, but there is no comfort in statistics.

Colleagues were kind, even generous, offering encouragement and thoughtful constructive criticism of the surgery and post-operative care. He absorbed it all and worked hard to better prepare himself for similar situations. Still, knowledge and absolution were different. The doubt lingered. Was he good enough? Would the community ever trust him again? Should he even continue to do this… or walk away?

93: The Experience

Brett and Casey sit side by side in an empty movie theater. The screen glows faintly in front of them. Their faces are still, their expressions numbed.

CASEY: "Are we there yet?"

BRETT: "Where?"

CASEY: "The good part?"

BRETT: "I don't know, I don't think so."

CASEY: "How will we know?"

BRETT: "They said we would enjoy it."

CASEY: "Said we *would* or *should*?"

BRETT: "I don't know."

CASEY: "Who even *are* they?"

BRETT: "The critics."

CASEY: "And why do we listen to them?"

BRETT: "Because…they know what is good for us?"

CASEY: "When was the last time the critics were actually right?"

BRETT: "I don't know."

CASEY: "Maybe we should just make our own choices."

BRETT: "Based on what?"

CASEY: "Our own preferences. We can't do any worse than the critics."

BRETT: "You don't know that; we could be worse."

CASEY: "Well, I haven't enjoyed a bit of this."

BRETT: "There's the end, guess we missed the good part. Now I'll have to see it all over again."

CASEY: "You can't be serious; there *was* no good part!"

BRETT: "Clearly, I wouldn't know. You were talking through the whole thing."

They sit in silence. The screen flickers one last time and fades to black.

94: Weeds

There is a legend that a young man was deeply in love with a beautiful maiden. He pursued her relentlessly. She stated that she required a sign that the gods favored the union. She proposed that they climb the mountain near their village in search of the lovely blue flowers that bloomed along the tree line. She would use them for her bouquet, which would signify that they were meant to be together.

They held hands and sang as they climbed up the steep trail. The temperature became colder, and her legs grew tired. The young girl could go no further. Her beloved trudged on alone, with the promise that he would not return without the periwinkles that she desired. She waited, but he never returned. Heartbroken, she never married. When she died, the townsfolk planted the blue flowers on her grave.

This is the tale that has been passed on for generations. To this day, young couples often choose to repeat the ritual. They climb the mountain to gather periwinkles for the bridal bouquet, demonstrating the approval of the gods for their marriage.

The truth is considerably less romantic, darker, and far more tragic. The young man was not the maiden's only suitor. She had a secret lover—one she chose with passion rather than promise. The girl lured her unsuspecting fiancé up the mountain and feigned exhaustion.

There, her lover ambushed and killed him. She returned down the hill with the tragic story that her fiancé was missing. Search parties found no trace of him. She mourned publicly and dramatically, playing her role to perfection.

In time, she moved to a nearby village "to escape the painful memories". There, she married her lover. Living with her secret, her beauty was slowly eroded by middle age.

Eventually, the fiancé's skeletal remains were discovered and revealed obvious evidence of murder. The villagers sought justice. The girl and her husband were tracked down. They were tried for murder. He was executed, and she died alone and forgotten in prison. Truth and fiction merge in the fact that her grave is covered with periwinkles, which grow like weeds in the prison cemetery.

95: Nonsense

He grimaced as he looked over his daily planner. The thought of meeting with the appropriations committee chair had already ruined his day. The woman was certifiably crazy. Just spending a few minutes with her would be enough to give him a "two-Tylenol, two-Advil" headache. He would have to remain calm and try to keep her focused. This was serious business. He promised himself a stiff shot of his favorite Ron Zacapa rum after this was over.

"Wouldn't you agree, Governor, that your budget proposal is like 'Trying to make a silk purse from spilled milk'?" she asked.

"Uh, I think you mean, 'Trying to make a silk purse out of a sow's ear,'" he replied sarcastically.

"No, that's not it, but let's not 'Make a mountain out of your chickens before they hatch,'" she shot back.

"I don't think that is how that saying goes …"

"Oh, I'm sure it is," she interrupted. "After all, as I've said so often, 'A penny saved is money well spent.'"

"That's not how any of those go," he muttered under his breath. Then, regaining composure, asked, "What is your point? We're still talking about the proposed budget, right?"

"Absolutely!" she said enthusiastically. "I'm a naturally curious person, you know. 'An idle mind gathers no moss.'"

"Okay … do you have specific concerns?" the Governor probed.

"I noticed that you have nothing budgeted for UFO defense."

"That would be because that is not a legitimate government expenditure. We have no UFO problem," he replied.

"But still, an ounce of prevention is worth a thousand words," she shot back.

"Here we go again," he thought. Certainly, no one would fault him if he just strangled her right now. Instead, he said, "Exactly what UFO deterrence would you recommend?"

"I'm no expert on that sort of thing. I suppose laser pointers would be a good starting point. Perhaps we should request a proposal from the National Guard. I just think we should have something budgeted so we aren't caught flat-footed when it happens."

The Governor, now fully losing it, face reddened, jugular veins bulging, exclaimed, "I suppose we should include funding for the zombie apocalypse as well."

"Now we're on the same page!" she shot back. "Let's talk about bitcoin."

"ARGHHHH!"

96: Voices

She couldn't remember when the voices started. They were angry and persistently nagged at her. She heard them alone in her home—even while driving. Everything seemed to be in crisis, and it was all her fault. The planet only had a few years to survive, the economy was collapsing, and even democracy itself was in peril. Adamant voices repeated, over and over, that she was a terrible, selfish, hateful person. She was beside herself with guilt and self-loathing.

She searched desperately for some escape, some end to the auditory harassment. It was then that she began to hear a second set of voices: softer, reassuring, comforting voices. These voices explained that everything was not her fault. Indeed, the crises were the natural ebb and flow of environmental, economic, and political cycles. History was replete with similar periods of adaptation and survival. Resilience was humanity's greatest strength. Things were going to be OK.

She tried to tell others to relax; there was no need to panic. She told them about the comforting voices and what they had told her. They did not believe her. How could she be so naïve as to believe such lies? They demanded she snap out of her dangerous denial of the crisis surrounding them. Refusing to resubmit to despair, they deemed her clearly beyond help. Her friends and family shunned her.

In her isolation, the calm voices continued to reassure her. Slowly, time passed without the major calamities that had been predicted. As one crisis faded, another arose. The angry voices persisted, but she had learned to separate out the hyperbole. She felt good about herself. The world remained uncertain but was no longer terrifying.

97: Special

Have you ever dreamed that you could fly? I mean really fly, not just flapping your arms like a bird. I'm talking about soaring above buildings and trees with arms stretched wide like wings. In my dreams, my hands somehow become a combination of aileron and elevator, controlling pitch and lift. Then I land on my feet like Superman. It is the greatest feeling.

When I stop and think about it, I have no idea what the propulsion system is. There is no rudder at all, but somehow it works.

Have you ever had a situation where you're not sure whether something really happened or you just dreamed it? You know, did you actually scratch your car, or just dream it? So, you go out and look at your car. Well, I became absolutely convinced that I could actually fly. I couldn't do it all the time, or even at will—just sometimes. I didn't know how, but I'm sure that I had done it.

I started experimenting, trying to do it again. Takeoffs were the biggest challenge. I was able to fly only a foot or two from the standing position. The landings were clumsy, more like stumbling than a graceful touchdown. It was better when I launched from a chair or the front porch. I worked my way up to a tabletop and felt that a second-floor window was the next logical step. That may have been a little too ambitious.

That particular takeoff was one of my best, as I was able to manage a near-horizontal position. The distance was good too, about ten feet. The landing, however, was considerably less successful than my previous attempts.

Dr. Barnett tells me I'm special. I disagree. I think a lot of us can fly; we just don't make the effort. You know how some people can play a song on the piano just by listening to it? That's exactly how I am with flying. It's a natural gift.

You may be like that too. You never know until you try. It is so exciting when it works! Let my success be your example—go for it!

As soon as I get out of the hospital, I'm going right back to practicing take-offs. Probably from a chair again at first, but I'm determined to get back to a second-floor window or maybe even a roof. Dr. Barnett tells me that walking is going to be difficult and that I'm going to need a lot of physical therapy. I'm not worried, though. Walking is not nearly as important when you can fly.

98: A Friend

She was sitting on the front porch, shelling peas, when he arrived—a scruffy little thing, no particular breed, with short brown fur and the most endearing smile. A mutt in search of a friend. Life on the farm could be lonely; the nearest children lived miles away. She needed a friend just as much as he did.

She named him Ralph Potato Leaf, though she only used his full name when he was in trouble.

From that moment, they were inseparable. He sat by her at meals, waiting for scraps. He slept at the foot of her bed, curling close on cold winter nights. They swam together in the pond, raced across the pasture with her pony, Toby, and spent long summer afternoons exploring the fields. She wound narrow strips of leather into a ball and taught Ralph to play fetch. He, in turn, did his best to help with chores, fetching sticks when she gathered firewood—though he always hesitated to let go.

Every morning, Ralph walked her to school, waiting in the yard until recess, when he could join the children at play. In the winter, when the snow was deep, he nestled under the schoolhouse, out of the wind, until she emerged at the end of the day.

As the years passed, boys began to notice her, but she always trusted Ralph's judgment. If he didn't like them, neither did she. Perhaps that's why she fell for Josh. Ralph adored Josh from the start, and in time, she and Josh became engaged. She imagined the three of them starting a new life together—Ralph as much a part of their future as he had been of her past.

But Ralph was growing older. Gray hairs framed his muzzle, his once-sharp teeth rounded, and his steps grew slower.

The day before her wedding, Ralph was nowhere to be found. Panic settled in as she scoured the farm, calling his name. She galloped through the fields on Toby, searching. Josh, Ma, and Papa joined in, but there was no trace of him. The eve of the most important day of her life, and her childhood best friend had vanished.

Papa found her sitting on the porch, worry etched across her face. He didn't have to say a word. Somehow, she already knew.

Ralph had always understood her, understood the changes in her life. And now, he understood that his time with her was over.

Tears slipped down her cheeks as she whispered his name into the night. She would never see Ralph again. Tenderly, Josh sat down beside her and caressed her hand. She leaned her head against his shoulder and opened her eyes.

99: Assholes

She fumed as another driver cut her off. Her road rage thundered. It didn't help that her mathematician jerk of a husband was taking pleasure in calculating the statistics of the situation.

"It could conservatively be estimated that 5-10% of the population will exhibit behavior that you might find objectionable. There are six lanes of bumper-to-bumper traffic all heading the same way. At 150 to 180 cars per lane per mile, that would mean that there are approximately 500 cars within a half mile both ahead and behind us. Hence, we are surrounded by 50 to 100 assholes," he cheerfully summarized.

"I'm seriously thinking of kicking the one beside me out onto the freeway," she shot back.

"Babe, I'm just saying that there are a lot of them out there."

"You're not helping," she snapped, her grip tightening on the steering wheel.

A horn blasted behind her, causing her to jerk in her seat. A large SUV was just inches from her rear bumper. She glared in the rearview mirror, memorizing the face of the driver.

"Back off, asshole!" she shouted into the mirror.

Immediately, the SUV decelerated and fell back to a safe distance.

"See what happens when you ask nicely?" her husband said recklessly under his breath.

She looked again and saw the flashing red and blue lights of a patrol car pulling the SUV over.

"One down, ninety-nine to go," she thought.

100: Tomorrow

There is no tomorrow without today. There is no today without yesterday. And so it goes: an endless cycle, without beginning or end. One day blurs into the next, a monotony void of hope. Yet, on a personal level, there is a definite beginning and an inevitable end. There lies the rub: we never know when that end will come.

She couldn't shake the thought.

Her cell offered no distractions, just the necessities stripped of even the pretense of comfort: a cot, a small commode, a cold-water sink, and a stand with a metal pitcher and cup. The walls were bare concrete, gray and unpainted, with a single towel bar. A barred window overlooked an empty exercise yard, hemmed in by towering walls crowned with razor wire. Beyond that were only perpetually overcast skies.

The iron door facing her window had a single sliding portal, just wide enough for a meal tray. She saw no other prisoners. Heard no voices. The silence was absolute. The solitude was a massive weight.

She thought back to how it had started. The words that had sealed her fate.

The judge had given her a chance to speak before sentencing. It was merely a formality, required by legal protocol. She should have remained silent, but that went against her nature.

"I've heard, over and over, that I am the most selfish, heartless person in the country," she had said with the defiance that had defined her entire life. "Well, I feel no remorse for what I've done. Lock me away forever. Quite honestly, I couldn't care less if I ever see or hear another human being again."

The judge had nodded slowly, as if the weight of her words made the harshness of his sentence easier to pronounce, "As you wish."

The guards who brought her meals were nameless figures in black hoods and gloves. They never made eye contact or spoke. They never touched her. The only skin she saw was her own. The only voice she heard was her own echoing off the concrete walls.

Her meals arrived with monotonous precision: oatmeal and tomato juice for breakfast; cabbage soup and a slice of bread for lunch; two small potatoes or turnips with greens and three chunks of pork or lamb for supper. The portions never varied. The temperature was always lukewarm.

Once, she had perused fine menus and contemplated wine pairings. Now, she brushed her teeth obsessively, desperate to scrub away the taste of greasy lamb.

Once, she had captivated audiences with her lectures and engaged in probing debate. Now, all her conversations were one-sided. The isolation was complete. Her only companion was her worst enemy.

Regret was pointless. Regret was weakness. And she was not weak.

She made her bed and lay down. Regardless of her defiant nature, yesterday, today, and tomorrow would be the same—forever.

101: The Calm

He woke up to a dark face on the digital clock. The power must be out. Sunlight streamed through the curtains of his beachfront rental. He threw on some shorts and sandals and headed for the beach. A dozen or so people were gathered, staring out at the sea.

"What's going on?" he asked. Then he noticed that there were no waves. The sea was eerily still—like a glass of water. He pulled out his cell phone to search for "dead calm", but there was no signal.

"There's no wind," someone said. "That might explain the waves, but where are the birds?"

The beach was unnervingly quiet. There were no gulls wheeling overhead or sandpipers skittering along the tide line. Aside from the group's murmurs, the only sound was breathing—shallow, fast, and suddenly noticeable.

He headed back for the bar to see if the TV was reporting anything strange. The bar was dark, and the bartender reported that she couldn't get the generator started.

"Anyone have a radio?" asked a female voice.

"Nothing but static," came a reply from someone in the growing crowd.

"I still have some ice, but it won't last long in this heat. I'd suggest everyone take advantage now before things start to warm up," the bartender advised.

That seemed like a good idea. Soon, the group gathered on the veranda, sipping cool drinks. The alcohol fueled a festive mood as strangers shared experiences with power outages and tropical misadventures.

Two tanned young men approached and reported that the jet skis and boats were not starting either.

"Must be one of those electromagnetic pulse things," someone offered.

"EMPs don't affect generators or small engines," countered another, an actual engineer.

"Whatever is going on, it is not going to ruin my day in paradise," volunteered an older lady, swirling her third vodka martini.

A young woman paced back and forth, anxiously fixated on her lifeless phone. "You do realize we are 40 miles from anything, and nothing seems to be working. This might seem less like paradise when the booze and food run out."

A firm voice declared, "There's no need to panic. We're safe here. The island will provide for us. People have lived here for centuries."

"What does that even mean?" the young voice asked sarcastically.

"Stranded here forever, with nothing to eat but coconuts and fish we have no means of catching?"

The now-tipsy older lady smiled mischievously, "Oh, honey, we could always eat you."

102: Night Watch

The private tugged back his sleeve and checked his watch. Green luminous hands pointing to two o'clock elicited a sigh of relief and a small cloud of vapor into the frigid air. He leaned over in the foxhole and cautiously nudged the sergeant awake.

"Your watch, Sarge," he whispered, barely audible.

Weapon cradled in his arms, the sergeant awoke with his heart suddenly racing. He slowly positioned himself at the ready and peered out over the rim of the foxhole. Without further communication, the private settled into a corner, closed his eyes, and surrendered to exhaustion.

The night was black, with a moonless, overcast sky. There was little difference between eyes open and eyes shut. The cold heightened the sergeant's anxiety. He was experienced enough to sense the danger. He shivered to keep warm, but the metallic taste in his mouth betrayed basic fear. The enemy was out there. Were they huddling to stay warm or advancing, hidden within the black expanse? He strained to detect anything—the slightest sound or indication of movement. There was nothing.

The private's mind drifted into a deep, dreamy sleep—he approached her from behind, standing fresh from her bath. He placed his hands gently on her shoulders and lingered over her neck. Leaning in, he softly kissed her, slowly moving from the nape down her spine. She shivered with arousal, leaning back against him. Responding, his heart quickened as he paused at the small of her back. He wrapped his arms around her waist, meeting her fingers at the navel. Now he pressed his face tenderly into her back as he tightened his grip. A deep sigh oozed from her lips...

PHFFFTHP! The sound—instantly familiar to any combat veteran—shattered the cold stillness.

The private's eyes snapped open, looking toward the sergeant. In that instant, he was aware of a faint form slumped to his side and a warm mist in the air. As he instinctively gasped, the air had a slightly salty taste.

PHFF... Then there was nothing.

103: Wyzetta

The doctor entered the exam room. "Good morning, Kara, how are you today?"

"Just fine, thanks."

"What brings you in today?"

"I wanted to ask if I should be taking Wyzetta?"

He was slightly taken aback. "I'm sorry, I'm not familiar with Wyzetta. What exactly is it?"

"I don't know. I saw a commercial on TV that said I should ask my doctor if Wyzetta was right for me."

"Kara, the only Wyzetta I've ever heard about is a town in Minnesota, but I think that is Wayzata. Do you have any idea what it is indicated for? Is it an over-the-counter supplement or a prescription medication?"

"I thought you would know all about it. They advertise it all the time on TV. The people who take it seem so happy."

The doctor's eyebrows rose, and his forehead wrinkled as he turned to his computer and typed.

"Here it is. Wyzetta may be beneficial for individuals who suffer from hippopotomonstrosesquippedaliophobia."

"What is that?"

"Hmm," he continued to type into his computer. "Apparently, it is the fear of mispronouncing long words." Now incredulous, he asked, "Are you experiencing any problems in that regard?"

"Well, I wouldn't want to try 'hippopotamus equestrian' or whatever you said."

"Chances are slim that it'll come up in your daily conversations," he replied in a bemused tone.

"Probably not, but just out of curiosity, do you think my insurance would cover it if I did ever need it?"

The doctor paused, then added farcically, "Possibly, if the prescription was written in Latin."

104: Loss

He drew me into an alley and revealed the truth. I was numb to what he was saying. His words did not sink in. It was as if he were speaking to someone else.

I shut out the message. It wasn't true. It couldn't be true. I sought to escape him and run from the truth.

He persisted, and my rage grew. I would not allow it. I thrashed against him to make him take it back. I could not prevail.

Perhaps there was an alternative. What were my options? Intelligent people can always work something out. Would he work with me? It became obvious that he was being unreasonable.

All was lost. There was no way out. All my hard work, my plans, and my dreams were for nought. Why did I even try? The game was rigged, and I was played for a fool.

What now? There have been others in my situation—this new normal. How do I move forward? I revisited my recent emotions, trying to make sense of the truth. He just looked at me, giving me space to come to terms with it.

So, this is it. This is the outcome. There's no going back. I understood the truth. He stepped aside. I walked toward the light.

105: Devil's Brew

The Devil hunched over a bubbling cauldron, mixing the bones of tortured souls into a thick, gelatinous goo. His minions brought him a disgusting mixture of celery, carrots, cucumbers, asparagus, fennel, peas, a lemon, and a hard-boiled egg. He stirred with his pitchfork, poured the concoction into a large bowl, and set it aside to cool.

When it was set, he turned the bowl upside down and slid the formed jelly onto a plate. Flies immediately fled the room. The Devil was pleased with his work.

"Now what?" his demons asked, delighting in the repulsive creation. The translucent dome contained vegetables suspended like insects trapped in amber, wobbling with each movement of the platter.

"We feed it to the damned," the Devil replied, savoring the cruelty of his words.

The minions exchanged worried glances. "With respect, Dark Lord, do we not have torture enough with the boiling oil, the searing fire, the perpetual remorse, the hopelessness—and Tuesdays with the Devil himself?" they questioned. "Surely this vile substance is beyond the pale."

The Devil's expression uncharacteristically softened. "Little ones,

I can't just rest on my laurels and let things get stale. Innovation is the key to keeping damnation fresh and relevant."

A minor demon in the back raised his hand. "Pardon me, if I might make a suggestion. Why not visit this atrocity upon the living as a new form of plague?"

Locusts escaped from the Devil's mouth as he laughed in glee, "Outstanding—brilliant! That is just what I shall do."

The minor demon, disguised as a sweet-faced grandmother, journeyed to Earth with the brew. She offered samples to unsuspecting mortals at county fairs and church socials, raving about its nutritional benefits and elegant presentation. Soon, the recipe was spread far and wide. It became a staple of holiday gatherings.

The Devil took great pleasure in seeing kindly old women torturing their families with aspic, as it came to be known. It was considered too vile to be fed to the tortured souls in Hell, yet it diabolically became a staple on the Thanksgiving and Christmas tables of the God-fearing.

To this day, small children innocently ask, "Why does grandma keep making that horrible aspic?"

Sadly, poor old grandma was tricked; the Devil made her do it.

106: Priorities

Ruby and Jack entered the clubhouse after a round of golf. They passed by the table where Lionel and Betty were sitting with several of their friends. They exchanged greetings and moved on to sit alone at a table across the room.

She felt somewhat awkward around Lionel. They had dated a few years before, and Ruby had dumped him for Jack.

The friends at Lionel's table were laughing and obviously having a good time. Ruby and Jack sat quietly, sipping their drinks and looking out at the golfers on the course. Occasionally, Jack would comment about a certain player's swing, but mostly they just sat in silence.

It had been different when she was with Lionel. She had always enjoyed his company, but she just couldn't get past the fact that he was not athletic. Golf and pickleball were very important to her. She was a talented athlete and wanted to be with someone who was athletic too. That was not Lionel. He tried, but his poor shots and lack of coordination embarrassed her.

Then there was his appearance. Ruby was still fit and very attractive. Lionel had been quite handsome in his youth, but now he was obese. She didn't understand why he wasn't concerned about his appearance. If he would only lose that weight, he would still be a nice-looking guy.

By contrast, Jack was extremely good-looking. He was an avid golfer and typically shot in the low 80s. On the pickleball court, he routinely played at the 4.5 level and won. Together, they made a striking couple.

She knew that Jack considered her to be quite a prize. In a way, she was a trophy wife, and if she allowed herself to be honest, Jack was her trophy husband. Yet, there she sat feeling alone, isolated, and bored. Their only interaction was Jack's occasional sarcastic quip about the perceived flaw in someone's golf game. For the first time in her life, she was envious of her friends…

Ruby suddenly got up and moved over to the other table.

"It looks like you guys are having all the fun at this table," she said. "Mind if I join you?"

She pulled up a chair, and within moments, she was engaged in the conversation. There was no talk of golf; only stories about travel, grandkids, food, and politics. They roared with laughter over the strange and embarrassing situations they had gotten themselves into. Each story seemed to top the last. There was good-natured teasing among longstanding friends. It was what clubhouses were for.

The waitress came by to refresh drink orders. Ruby noticed that when the waitress approached Jack's table, he looked up and, for the first time, noticed that she was missing.

Out of the corner of his eye, Jack spotted Ruby across the room. With a grin and a slight nod in her direction, he ordered another scotch and soda.

107: A Tree

At nearly 200 feet tall and 250 years old, Clarence stood among hundreds of close relatives—roots entangled, lives intertwined. He was a Ponderosa pine, fixed on a steep slope in a remote and quiet corner of the forest. For at least a decade, Clarence had noticed his footing growing increasingly precarious as erosion ate away the soil beneath him. He had even started to lean, ever so slightly, toward the downhill slope.

Years ago, he had witnessed his cousin Simone take a tumble when her roots could no longer support her. It was a loss that the family still struggled with. Clarence was worried that, like Simone, his age was catching up with him.

Dark clouds gathered in the southwest. A gentle rain began to fall, its drops intercepted by the forest canopy. But the rain did not stop. After two days, the soft drizzle had become a steady, unrelenting force. The soil became saturated and weak.

Clarence could see no end to the rain, and a sense of dread settled over him. He felt an almost imperceptible shift. Then, slowly, it escalated into a pronounced lean. He knew the end was near. With what time he had left, he marveled at the view he had for so long taken for granted. He gazed upon his cousins standing tall, a mist weaving between them. He made his peace with the inevitable. His family stood a solemn vigil at his side.

The final blow was sudden and violent. He landed in a heap and slid a small distance down the slope—his branches shattered, his roots torn and exposed.

The area was isolated, with no humans around. No woodland creatures to bear witness. He fell in silence.

So, there you have it—the answer to the age-old question:

If a tree falls in the forest and no one (or creature) is there to hear it, does it make a sound?

Clarence says no.

And he should know—he fell.

108: The Funeral

Petra was big, one name big. His death announcement interrupted live TV and was a bold print banner across cable and streaming networks. The funeral had to be produced with all the expertise of a major Hollywood Studio film. Only the best funeral planner would do. That, of course, was Sharlamaign—also one name big.

Fitting with their ego and stature within the funeral planner profession, Sharlamaign (pronouns: they/them) didn't wait for the call. They were a virtual tsunami of gender fluidity. They immediately got to work on the details. The William Andrews Clark, Jr. Mausoleum at Hollywood Forever Cemetery was fittingly ostentatious and must be booked. The LA Philharmonic's string section would be secured for a studio-composed soundtrack. That televangelist from Houston would be contacted to conduct the service.

They jotted down a list of six possible eulogists. There would be fellow Academy Award winners, his long-time agent, and of course, the defense attorney from the "trial of the century". Billy Grant was Petra's BFF, but was strictly banned from speaking after the fiasco at Ward Galante's service, where he mixed up Scientology and Mormonism and alienated a third of the A-listers.

The structure was a massive Ionic Greek Temple, elegant in

Georgia White Marble. The perfect venue for a live broadcast and possibly even an extended pay-per-view theatrical release. Seating, of course, was high priority to ensure that the blocking of each shot provided just the right balance of star power and DEI cred.

The current wife and legitimate children would be seated in the front row on the right side. Former wives and unacknowledged children would be in the first two rows on the left side. Fortunately, wives' number two and five each check the boxes for three DEI categories by themselves.

Eulogists and their plus ones would be seated in the second row on the right, followed by major award winners, lesser award winners, and B-listers. Siblings and out-of-town family members would be encouraged to view the live-stream in the Temple narthex.

The dress rehearsal went off with only minor adjustments. Fortunately, Sharlamaign remembered past problems with Emme Taylor's pocket dog and Simone Dupre's comfort pig and separated their seats by several rows.

Also, the original script had called for a CGI Petra to rise from his casket and serve as one of the pallbearers. However, the attorneys had somehow neglected to include this use in the NIL licensing agreement and it had to be cut.

NDAs were signed, A-list gift bags were arranged, product placement was meticulously sight-lined, and merchandising tables stocked. Everything was a go.

There was buzz about a near-certain Emmy nomination. A gauntlet of cosplay characters from Petra's most iconic roles formed along the red carpet as the limousines lined up for the opening. This would be Petra's finest moment.

109: Teamwork

She loved living in the country. Each day, she rode her bike fifteen to twenty miles on roads where she seldom encountered another vehicle. The wide-open spaces, mountain views, and expansive sky were nirvana to her.

It troubled her that even out here, the city was encroaching—not structurally, but through regulations. The hypocrisy of it was staggering. This was an open-range state. This meant that cattle legally had the freedom to roam wherever they chose. If you didn't want cattle in your yard, you had to **fence them out.** However, if you had a pet dog, the county required you to **fence it in.**

Put another way, if a bull mauled your child in your yard, it was **your fault** for not fencing the bull out. On the one hand, the dog owner is responsible for his pet; on the other, the rancher is not responsible for their cattle.

She understood this to be the collision of the historic and the modern. The open range was a concept born in the Old West that continues to this day. It allows cattle to graze on public lands and be moved from one place to another with minimal obstacles. The domestic pet restrictions arise from city folks—people with no concept of open space or freedom—who impose their limited view of the world on their country cousins. She understood the need to control pets in a densely populated area, but felt pets should enjoy "open range" rules outside the city.

She was still mulling over the absurdity of trying to regulate pets in the countryside when she approached a farmstead with two adorable St. Bernard puppies. They were about six months old, and she had been enjoying watching them grow up. They had a fenced yard, but the puppies were adept escape artists. Each day, they came out to greet her, slowing her down for fear of running into them.

This particular day, only one puppy scurried out. Blocking her path and causing her to come nearly to a stop. Just then, the second puppy darted out from behind and bit her on the butt. She laughed at how they had coordinated their attack. These were smart dogs, and she'd fallen right into their trap.

"You little devils," she said, softly chuckling. "You know, I could sue your owner."

Tomorrow, she'd be ready for their tricks.

Out here, every day was an adventure.

110: Unacceptable

Victoria was not pleased. The principal had called and requested an immediate conference regarding her daughter's behavior. She had a full schedule and could not understand why the principal insisted she come personally rather than sending her assistant. This was unacceptable.

She arrived at the school with a hair-trigger temper. Whatever was going on was going to end quickly. She did not have time to waste on a petty, self-important administrator.

"What is this all about?" she demanded as she entered the principal's outer office.

"Please come in, Ms. Kretchmar," the principal said in a somewhat bemused tone from within her private office.

Victoria strode vigorously into the office where the principal sat behind her desk and Willow sat in one of two side chairs.

"Please have a seat."

"I prefer to stand. Precisely why am I here?"

"Willow, please explain your situation to your mother."

"Mother, after careful consideration, I have chosen to end my relationship with Mrs. Leahy. This has not been an easy decision. We entered our relationship with the expectation that it would last the entire school year, but irreconcilable differences have arisen that necessitate a personal uncoupling. We will always love and respect each other, but we cannot continue on our life path together. I ask for your understanding and respect for our privacy at this difficult time. Please refrain from further questions or judgment."

"I don't understand what the problem is."

The principal paused to carefully suppress a smirk. "Well, Ms. Kretchmar, we do not allow second graders to 'divorce' their teachers."

"Certainly, a child should be allowed to change teachers if there is conflict," Victoria shot back.

"Willow, why don't you clarify for your mother what the 'conflict' is with Mrs. Leahy."

"Mother, she is quite unreasonable. She expects me to have completed my assignments regardless of my evening agenda," Willow earnestly explained.

"This seems straightforward to me. Will you grant her request?"

"No," the principal replied.

"Then, I have no recourse but to immediately withdraw Willow from Sandstone Academy," Victoria announced.

"*Thank you, Lord,*" the principal thought as a subtle smile creased her face.

111: Last Game

Stains studied the two-inch white tape on the visitor's locker at Fenway—his last name and uniform number, nothing more. But that said it all. He knew he was lucky to have even that. If the tape had read, "Good glove, no hit," everyone would still have known it was his. Six Rawlings Bill Doak model gloves had kept him in the majors for a thousand games over sixteen seasons with seven second-division teams. Solid middle infield defense had trumped a lifetime .252 batting average with no power. Today, his journey would end with the Washington Senators and the final game of the 1952 season. Well-liked and dependable, he would leave no mark on the game.

Bucky had pulled him aside after Saturday's game. It was not his job, but a courtesy to a veteran player. Stains appreciated the heads up. Cal had decided to release him at the end of the season. This was neither a surprise nor something new for a journeyman like Stains. The Pirates cut him two years ago, and Bucky had invited him to spring training to compete for a spot at second base. Now he was nearly forty and would not go through that again. He had no interest in battling it out with the next young stud, whose value rested solely on the ability to pull line drives into the left-field stands. $4,200 was probably more than he would ever earn again, but it was time to get a real job. One last game, and then move on.

Early in his career, Stains hated the wool/flannel blend uniforms. They were heavy and uncomfortable. In the last two years, new synthetic blends had made their way to even the lowly Senators. That change had made the dog days of late July and August bearable. Now it was the cool of September, and he almost missed the warmth of the old fabric. He pulled on a long-sleeved undershirt, tucked in his jersey, and fastened his pants. His shoes wore the scars of a season's wear. He laced them up, grabbed his cap and glove, and stepped out to the dugout.

He sat on the bench between Pete and Mickey, three veteran friends looking forward to the end of a long season. His career would end on the field. Bucky had penciled him in at second in place of Holderlein. He would bat seventh. The Senators ended the top half of the first with Jensen stranded at first, typical of this year's struggles.

Stains climbed the steps and jogged to second base. Mickey tossed him some infield grounders. Then came the call, "balls in, coming down". Masterson threw his last warm-up pitch, and Grasso drilled the peg to Pete covering second. Stains shifted to the edge of the outfield grass behind second for backup. Then returned to his position.

Lipon stepped up to the plate for the Red Sox. Stains shifted his weight onto the balls of his feet and leaned into position. He was confident and relaxed.

"Please, Lord, let him hit it to me."

9 781968 745165